THE RIDER IN THE NIGHT

Also by Brendan Noble

The Frostmarked Chronicles:
A Dagger in the Winds

The Prism Files:
The Fractured Prism
Crimson Reigns
Pridefall
White Crown

For my amazing wife, Andrea, who has encouraged me and tolerated my endless rants about Slavic mythology.

Major Gods and Their Marks

Marzanna - Frostmark
Winter, Disease, and Death

Dziewanna - Bowmark
Wilds, Hunt, and Spring

Jaryło - Springmark
Spring, Agriculture, and War

Mokosz - Mothermark
Women and Divination

Perun - Thundermark
Thunder, Justice, and War

Weles - Serpentmark
Underworld and Lowlands

Swaróg - Forgemark
Celestial Fire and Smithing

Dadźbóg - Sunmark
The Sun

Pronunciation Guide

Major characters

Andrij Myroslavovych Yakymchuk: Ahndrey
      Mihrohslahvohvihch Yahkihmchuhk

Valentyn: Vahlehnteen

Mykyta: Mihkeeta

Oleh: Ohleh

Boz Vladyslavovych Kramarenko: Bohz
      Vlahdihslahvohvich Krahmahrehnkoh

Beáta: Behahtah

Major Gods

Marzanna: Mahrzahnah

Dziewanna: Djehvahnah

Jaryło: Yahrihwoh

Mokosz: Mohkohsh

Perun: Pehruun

Weles: Vehlehs

Swaróg: Svahrohg

Dadźbóg: Dahdzbohg

Strzybóg: Strihbohg

Other Terms

Kynnytsia: Kihnihtseeah

Dwie Rzeki: Dvee Zehkee

Małe Wzgórze: Mahweh Vzgohzeh

Krowik(ie): Krohvihk(ee)

Astiw(ie): Ahstihv(ee)

Solga(wi): Sohlgah(vee)

Zurgow(ie): Zuhrgowv(ee)

Simuk(ie): Sihmuhk(ee)

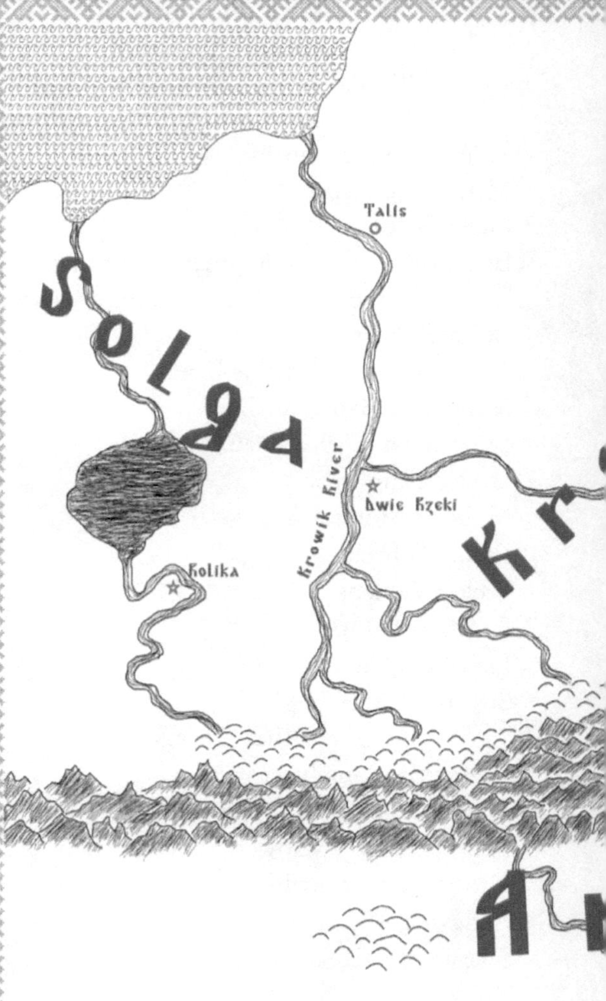

Solga
Talis
Krowik River
Dwie Rzeki
Kr
Holika
A

Klist
Mangled Woods
Simuk
Clan Encampment
Wik
Wyzra River
Narrow Pass
ałe Wzgörze
Kynnytsia
Astiw
Zurgow
uthern Hills
Vastroth
Huebia
vora
Télem

PREQUEL TO THE FROSTMARKED CHRONICLES

THE RIDER IN THE NIGHT

BRENDAN NOBLE

1

A harsh chill blew over the peaks of Perun's Crown and swept across the scattered trees of spruce and pine. Andrij shivered, pulling his furs tight over his shoulders.

Why did I have to speak up?

King Boz hadn't responded well to his suggestion to place a spare rooster or two in each of the threshing houses in case the ovinniks got the wrong idea at winter's end. The blasted demons had burned down three in in the surrounding villages already. But Boz never took kindly to ideas—other than his own.

Guarding the trail through the Narrow Pass was an easy station for a warrior during the summer. Now, though, during the waxing Marzec moon, Andrij could barely feel the tips of his fingers beneath his woolen gloves.

His mother would've scolded him for not wearing an extra layer. Luckily, she was in his home village of Khakovo, far from the mountain winds.

Andrij hoped his mother was warm, huddled with his six siblings around their cottage's stove. After all she'd suffered, he wished he'd been able to provide more. Though he had done his best on the farm with her for twelve years, that'd been before the king had come to collect his late father's debt, forcing Andrij to become a guard.

It had been five years since Boz's warriors had torn him, yelling and kicking, away from his widowed mother and starving family. He hadn't seen them since.

He sighed, creating a puff of fog that was barely visible in the moonlight. *Just a week until the spring equinox,* he reminded himself, but that hope of warmth felt distant during the long night.

Another gust of wind slipped through Andrij's gloves, and he swore as his fingers grew numb against his spear's wooden staff. The cold wouldn't have been so bad if he'd had Mykyta's humor or even Valentyn's old stories of battles against the nomadic clans from the east. Instead, he was alone with the cries creeping through the cliffs high above.

Many of the other guards had spoken of the voices in the Narrow Pass when he'd first arrived.

Andrij hadn't believed them, but since then, he'd spent many nights guarding the eastern trail. It sounded like a woman's scream at times. Others, it reminded him of a serpent hiding in the brush.

Hours passed slowly, but Andrij let himself smile when the golden light of Dadźbóg, god of the sun, finally crested the peaks. With the lifeless sea of white around him no longer shrouded in darkness, his fear and exhaustion faded. Soon, another guard would replace him. He could remove his boots, slurp down some lukewarm soup, and drop into his bed. It wasn't much, but the thought of sleeping until late afternoon, uninterrupted, was the only thing keeping him sane.

Then the ground began to shake.

Instinct took over. Andrij flipped his shield off his back and gripped his spear, wriggling his fingers to bring some feeling back into them. Unfortunately, the only sensation that followed was a dull throb from the cold.

"Halt!" he shouted, though his voice was little more than a squeak.

The sound of horses galloping through the snow approached, unrelenting. Two of them, Andrij approximated. There was a slim chance he could fight them, but he would never make it back to Kynnytsia to alert the others in time. *Gods, why did he have to send me alone tonight?*

"Halt!" he tried again to no avail. His lip quivered and his breaths were raspy, but Andrij forced himself to hold his ground. If the clans finally had the guts to attack the Astiwie capital, he wasn't going to be the first to flee—just the first to fall.

The first rider tore down the trail, his bay horse huffing at full gallop and his tan cloak flapping behind him. His gaze was fixed on Andrij.

Andrij waited for the horseman to draw within a spear's length, just like Valentyn had taught him. When the next rider swarmed from his other flank, though, his footing failed. He stumbled and dropped to a knee as the attackers advanced, their frames casting a cold shadow over him.

They spoke between themselves in a quick tongue unlike anything he'd heard. Warriors from villages further north had described the eastern clansmen as beasts with spiraled horns that sowed destruction and massacred innocents, but the riders before him appeared to be merely a dark-skinned man and woman—one of each.

"Who are you?" Andij asked.

The tan-cloaked man grinned and drew down his hood, revealing his curled black hair. "I am Bidaês of Clan Simuk, eldest grandson of Marzban Katiôn," he said in the Astiwie tongue, "and this is—"

"You do not speak for me," the woman snapped. "You may call me Zhaleh, messenger of Clan Zurgow and priestess of Otlezd." She left her hood up, but Andrij eyed the green line of paint arcing above her furrowed brow. *They have female warriors?*

Bidaês rolled his eyes but continued, "We come with an offer for your king."

"Our… Our king?" Andrij mumbled, examining the man. He rode tall with his chin held high, but his voice was young, and Andrij guessed he was no older than himself.

"Yes," Bidaês said with a sigh. "Show him to us, or we will find the way ourselves."

The girl scoffed and muttered something Andrij didn't understand, but he'd heard enough. The riders would reach Kynnytsia whether he showed them or not. *Boz won't like that.* The king despised most people, and Andrij doubted these uninvited foreigners would be any different. He winced at the thought. *If he doesn't kill me, he'll have me shoveling manure for weeks.*

Andrij rose and steadied his breaths. "I will show you the way, but allow me to enter the village first. Your presence will startle our warriors."

Bidaês laughed with a hand on the hilt of his curved sword. "If your warriors are anything like yourself, we should have few issues."

"Follow me, then." Andrij backed away, feeling even smaller than he had before. "I will show you where it is safe to wait."

They both nodded, and he led them down the steep slope. From here, many of the rolling hills within Astiwie lands were visible. Marzanna, goddess of winter and death, ruled them all for now. Come the equinox, though, the Jaryło—god of spring and war—would slay her and bring life to the crops and nature. Dadźbóg's full light would then cast a golden dawn over the forests and plains. Andrij had anticipated that day for many moons. With two clan riders at his back, however, that hope faded.

Kynnytsia was nestled among the trees and hills an hour's hike from Andrij's guard post. It was the largest village in the tribe, yet even from this elevation, Andrij could barely make out the scattered cottages. In fact, the only clear building was King Boz's circular home at the peak of the highest hill.

"Your people live here all their lives?" Bidaês asked as they passed the first fields and homes.

Andrij, still rigid from his shock, forced himself to nod.

"And what if there is little to eat? Surely you cannot forage for enough in one place for so long?"

"Mother always said Jaryło blesses our crops," Andrij replied. "Our lands have never been barren, and as far as I know, we've never moved from the shadow of Perun's Crown."

Zhaleh shook her head. "You speak of gods that do not exist. Only Otlezd and his six Uzeša Teṇpa protect the earth. If your people have found food plentiful, it is because of their giving."

"All I know is the stories Mother and the priests tell." Andrij paused and glanced back as the riders sneered at the single room cottages. "What offer do you have for the king? You should know he isn't a fan of talking."

Another smirk crossed Bidaês's face. "That reminds me of a *certain* high priestess."

"High Priestess Rasa is Otlezd's voice to our people," Zhaleh replied, eying the dagger at her side. "Speak ill of her again and I will slice off your fingers."

Noted.

"We come with a warning," she continued, turning her attention back to Andrij. "A great Horde has swept across the Anshayman Steppe. We have lost many to their arrows tipped with bone, and we intend to travel through your lands to evade them. Your king has two choices: allow us to pass or die."

Andrij swallowed. "Oh…"

"And this is why I was supposed to do the talking," Bidaês muttered. "Zhaleh puts it in unnecessarily harsh terms. We don't intend to harm your people, but if we are forced to face you or the Horde, we will choose you."

Is that supposed to make it any better?

Bidaês's attempt at reassurance hadn't stopped the churning of Andrij's stomach, but he faked a smile. The king would be furious when he heard their demand. All Andrij could hope was that he wasn't in the room when it happened.

The sun hung high above by the time they reached the place where the crossroads met. Andrij eyed the southern one—the trail home. Someday, he promised himself he would return to his mother and feel her soft embrace. This was not the day.

"Can you wait here?" Andrij asked the riders, considering if he should add "please" at the end to avoid Zhaleh's wrath.

The priestess waved a dismissive hand. "Be quick, and do not bring warriors to attack us. Our clans will march west whether we return or not."

Andrij nodded and took the center trail, passing more cottages as he passed through the wooden gate and neared the village center. Here, men gathered to sharpen their hunting spears, and old women with their patterned headscarves watched their grandchildren run amok. A few of them slipped across the trail, only missing Andrij's legs by half-a-stride. He chuckled at the scolding that followed. Life had never been easy for Andrij. Being a boy with an imaginative mind, though, had ensured his childhood had no lack of heroic battles against cattle or bundles of wheat, always drawing his mother's ire.

When he reached the circular clearing that marked the village center, he coughed from the stench of the tannery. King Boz had allowed it to be built four hundred strides to the west— upwind. No one had taken a breath of fresh air in Kynnytsia since.

Andrij felt the gaze of the king's guards as he approached Boz's home atop the hill. He'd returned from the Narrow Pass too soon, and they would surely whisper to the other warriors.

"I urgently need to speak with the king," he said, stopping before them with his hand tight around his spear. *Please make this easy.* He knew better. As one of the youngest of Boz's forced recruits, Andrij needed to prove himself at every opportunity. This one would be no different.

Ostap, the bulkier of the guards, stepped forward. "You can pass the message on with us."

Andrij matched his glare. "There are clan riders here who have a deal… or I guess a threat… that he will want to hear."

"You brought them *here?*" Ostap swapped glances with the other guard, Dmytro. "You better tell him then. I'd rather not die."

Dmytro's eyes widened, and he backed away, shaking his head. "No, I'm fine letting Andrij do it."

Wonderful…

Andrij took a sharp breath and pulled open the door to the house. Inside, the heat stung his frosted skin, but he ignored it as he passed down the narrow hall, lined with bear pelts upon the dirt floor. He'd never understood the king's obsession with killing any bear near the settlement; though, he had heard Boz mumbling about the bear-god Weles under his breath more than once. Each time one was spotted, the warrior on duty was required to go directly to the king. Then, Boz always insisted on slaying the beast himself.

At the end of the hall, the space widened into a circular room floored with more pelts, but King Boz's most prized kill hung behind his throne—the dragon-like demon the priests had called an aspid. Its hide was draped across the entire back wall with arrays of purple and gray dancing across the scales.

Andrij thought it would have been a magnificent beast to see with his own eyes, but Boz had hated its presence in the mountains. With a team of warriors, he'd slayed the aspid seven moons before, taking a few of its scales for his crown and its bones for his throne.

The king sat upon this throne, holding a clay mug and fixing his deep brown eyes upon Andrij. A cape of blue, trimmed in gold, draped from his shoulders. Though his hair had receded half-way up his scalp, no one dared to mention his age.

Andrij knelt at the room's entrance and waited for his king to speak. Silence reigned for a minute, and sweat collected on his brow. *What have I done? He's probably deciding how to punish me for abandoning my post.*

"Andrij," Boz began, his voice like that of a snake, "You come at the most inopportune time."

"I apologize, my king, but—"

Boz shot to his feet, throwing away his mug and spewing the liquid across a pelt. "Did I ask you to speak?" He stormed across the room and grabbed Andrij's ear. "I give you an opportunity away from that puny farm and you repay me by leaving your assignment?"

Andrij winced as his ear throbbed, but he knew better than to talk back. Everyone knew King Boz was cruel. Few, though, understood what his collection of guards did.

He was insane.

"Answer me!" Boz snapped before slamming Andrij's head into the dirt and stepping back.

"I… I…" Andrij tried to speak, but fear and the pounding of his head drowned every word.

The king huffed and eyed the guards along the rim of the room. "You smirk? Why? None of you are better than him!"

"The clansmen," Andrij stuttered, kneeling once again. "My king, messengers from the clans of Simuk and Zurgow have arrived with a warning."

Boz's eyes narrowed. "They dare cross the Narrow Pass to *talk* after all the villages they have raided in the north? What is the warning?"

"It may be best if they tell you."

The backhand caught Andrij off-guard, and his cheek stung as Boz scowled and returned to his throne. "You allowed clan riders into Kynnytsia—into *my* settlement?"

Andrij stared at the ground. *I'm dead.* "My king, they said they would carry out the worst of their plans if they didn't speak to you. I thought—"

"I do not care about your thoughts." He looked to a guard along the wall, "Bring them."

The guard nodded and jogged down the hall as Andrij shook his head. "But my king, I—"

"Have not learned your lesson apparently." Boz drummed his fingers on the bone armrests of his throne. "You will listen quietly during the meeting. Then I will decide what I want to do with you."

"Yes, my king."

2

"King Boz, I presume?" Bidaês said without a bow at the throne room's entrance. "My name is Bidaês of Clan Simuk, grandson to Marzban Katiôn." He still held a cocky smirk, and Andrij, from his kneeling position along the side wall, wondered if his cheeks hurt from holding it like that for so long.

Boz studied the visitors, clicking his tongue. Then, he stood and rounded his throne to the aspid hide. "Do your people have stories of dragons, 'Bidaês of Clan Simuk'?" he asked.

"Not of the air, but there are many stories of what lives beneath the dry ground of the steppe."

"There is one," Zhaleh interrupted. "Alunam, the devil, appears as a dragon that scorches the earth with his flames, and only Otlezd's—"

Boz's laughing tore across the room. The priestess fell silent, but her eyes were like daggers. "And who in Weles are you, girl?" Boz asked.

Zhaleh clenched her fists and stalked forward. "I am priestess Zhaleh of Clan Zurgow, second only to—"

"Adorable, the clans sent a zealous priestess and a boy to threaten me." Boz turned back to see her in the middle of the room. "You are quite easily angered, Zhaleh. Is it not in Otlezd's teachings to respect a man when he is speaking?"

Zhaleh growled, but before she could act, Bidaês grabbed her arm. "King Boz," he said. "We come from our clans with a message—one that petty insults will not delay."

"Speak, then, and make it good. My warriors are prepared to slit your throats should I not be entertained."

Bidaês cast Andrij a raised brow before returning his gaze to the king. "Very well, I will be quick." He told Boz the same story he'd told Andrij, adding a list of clans Andrij had never heard of that had been destroyed by the Horde.

When Bidaês finished, Boz's face was red, and his lip twitched. *He's going to execute them,* Andrij thought. *And I'll be next.*

"You speak like you haven't raided our villages for years," Boz said as he sat on his throne. "Your horsemen would be ripe for slaughter attacking through the Narrow Pass, and I would enjoy watching each of them fall."

"We have not done so," Bidaês insisted. "I cannot claim the same for the Zurgowie."

Zhaleh winced.

"Your clans are no different," Boz sneered. "Raiders, filthy nomads. You would rather take our lands than defend your own. Come and meet our spears. I'll impale your head on my own."

Zhaleh tapped the center of her chest and then slid her finger down to her stomach. "In Otlezd's name, you will suffer for this."

"And Perun's ax will strike you down like all others who dared cross the Narrow Pass!" Boz shouted, pointing to the doors. "Get out before I send my own messengers with nothing but your decapitated heads."

"We will give you until the first day of the moon you call Kwiecień to reconsider," Bidaês said. "Find us northeast of the Narrow Pass." Then, he left with Zhaleh.

Andrij let out a breath. He'd been recruited for war, and ferocity in battle would bring him honor. Yet, he was afraid of facing the clans. If the stories were right, they could defeat an army of twice their number. He would fight to protect his tribe, to protect the family he'd been torn from, but as he watched the duo leave, he wondered if he would ever see home again.

Boz paced around the room, muttering as Andrij prayed to Perun, god of thunder and justice, to protect him. It was among the god's mountains that his night had gone awry in the first place. Would Perun's mighty ax protect him from Boz's wrath?

It was a long time before the king sat on his throne and snapped his gaze to Andrij. "Come here," he ordered.

Without a word, Andrij rose and shuffled to the king. Boz watched him the entire way, and Andrij's skin crawled as he knelt before the throne.

"You are Death's messenger," Boz said, his voice sharp. "So, you will continue his work."

Andrij shook his head. "I don't understand."

"Let me finish!" the king hissed. "Those nomads will return with their armies, and, together, they could be too much for our warriors. Ready a horse for you, Valentyn, and that buffoon Mykyta. You ride for Dwie Rzeki immediately."

Dwie Rzeki? What does the Tribe of Krowik have to do with this?

"I see the question in your eye," Boz continued. "Let's just say High Chief Jacek owes me a favor after I saved him from the axes of Solga. Go to him and demand he bring his men to our defense, just as I have done for him."

Andrij bowed his head as an ache gripped his chest. "Yes, my king, but Dwie Rzeki is a week's ride if we push hard. It is likely we will reach them around the Drowning of Marzanna."

Boz leaned forward, eyeing him. "I'm counting on you arriving during the equinox festival. Jacek's chiefs will be gathered, and he will look weak if he rejects my call. He is an untrustworthy maggot, but he is my sister's husband. Natasza can be quite persuasive."

"I will ride, my king." *With no sleep.*

"Good. Now go. If you return, then I will take it as a sign from the gods that you have repaid your father's debt. If you don't, well, then you will have suffered Perun's punishment for your failure to remain at your post."

With a swift bow, Andrij fled the room and rushed back into the sunlight. He took a deep breath, enjoying its warmth on his face as fatigue swept across his body. *No rest until sundown. Perun give me strength, so that I may see Mother again, so that*

I may be free. That hope was enough to push him on.

Ostap huffed at the sight of him. "Huh. Guess the king is in a good mood today."

"I wouldn't bet on it," Andrij mumbled, wandering toward Boz's pastures just beyond the village center.

How was he to ride across nearly all of Astiwie and Krowikie lands in a week? There were few trails, and snow still covered the ground. Andrij had never left his tribe's lands, but Valentyn would know the way. The old warrior had fought both among the mountains of Perun's Crown and the swamps around the Krowik River. If there was anyone Andrij wanted on the journey, it was him.

The *caw* of a stray crow floated through the air. Each flap of its wings hammered Andrij's mind as he dreaded the rough, uncomfortable journey ahead. It was an unspoken truth that demons lurked in the forests at night. Around Kynnytsia, the gods' chosen sorceresses known as szeptuchy kept them at bay, but beyond the scattered villages of the twin tribes, attacks were common. His mother had always said those who wander alone into the woods after dusk rarely returned. *At least I won't be alone.*

The horses scattered as Andrij opened the pasture gate. Most did every time, choosing to stay near the hay and water trough instead of letting him rein them in for training. That didn't offend Andrij. He didn't need to be the stallions' friend, just their master, but he had broken that rule with one.

A dark bay horse with a patch of white along its front right shoulder trotted to him with a snort. Andrij smiled and rubbed Oleh's soft, droopy nose. Though he was awkward to ride and far too curious for his own good, Oleh had become a safe place. The stallion was gentle but stubborn at times, and, in a way, Andrij was thankful that he'd been forced to break him.

Learning to fight on horseback had been one of the more difficult periods in Andrij's training, but Oleh had gone through it with him. Valentyn believed them to be an odd pair. Andrij was just happy to have a trustworthy friend.

After slipping the bridle on Oleh's head, Andrij tied him to a post near the gate and went for the other horses. Valentyn would want Viktor, a massive black horse that had claimed alpha status in the pasture a long time ago. Viktor also hated Andrij, and when he approached the stallion, it huffed and bolted away.

Andrij sighed. *And this will be the easiest part of the trek.*

For half-an-hour, he scrambled around the pasture, out of breath when he finally wrangled both Viktor and Kazymyr, Mykyta's runt of a horse. He brought both of them to the fence as a deep laugh came from the trail ahead.

"Old Vitya give ya trouble?" Valentyn asked, leaning his stout frame against the wooden fence.

The blue cloak of an Astiwie veteran draped down Valentyn's shoulders with its hood covering his brown hair and beard. Take away the beard and he would have looked like an older, shorter version of Andrij—round cheeks, strong chin, and uncomfortably thick eyebrows. When Valentyn had taken Andrij under his wing a year before, he'd claimed to see himself in his apprentice. Now, Andrij wondered how literal that sentiment was.

Andrij grinned against his will as he tied up the horses. "No more than you do."

"Oh, I wouldn't do that to ya," Valentyn replied. "Especially not after Boz gave you the old knuckles to the cheek."

"You heard?"

" 'bout us going west? Half the village knows already." Valentyn pulled open the gate and

grabbed hold of Viktor's reins. "For your face…
Well, it ain't just red from the cold."

Andrij held his hand to his numb cheek as the
smell of smoke overwhelmed him. *He's been
smoking that stuff again.* Valentyn had complained
about his back pain for as long as Andrij had
known him. Then, a szeptucha of Weles—the
god of the lowlands and underworld—had given
him a plant with instructions to light it on fire and
inhale the vapors. With Boz's hatred of the god's
followers, Valentyn had kept it a secret from all
except Andrij, but he hadn't moaned about the
aches since. Still, he never seemed completely
present when the smoke hung over him.

Valentyn slapped his back. "You'll be fine, kid.
Boz ain't the softest, but things were worse
before 'im. Trust me."

*Worse than people starving because of the king's
unwillingness to handle the ovinniks?* Andrij gritted his
teeth. There had been reports of whole villages
abandoning their lands to find food. *Only a few
roosters would've tamed the demons…*

As Andrij opened his mouth to reply, Mykyta
strolled down the trail, swinging his arms more
than necessary and beaming from ear to ear.
"Heya Valentyn!" he exclaimed.

"Mykyta," Valentyn mumbled back.

"Thanks for getting Kazymyr for me!" Mykyta said as he hopped the fence, drawing another groan from the old warrior.

Andrij crossed his arms and held up his chin. "Actually, I caught all three of them."

Pausing, Mykyta examined him before patting his horse's neck. "I don't believe you. You're slower than Babay without his cane."

Andrij shuddered at the thought of the dark spirit. Most thought Babay, a crooked old man who haunted the forest, was just a tale to scare children, but those stories had never left his mind.

"And you're stupider than a Simukie rider without his horse," Valentyn snapped back. "Now shut yer mouth and let me get ready in peace." He pulled Viktor through the open gate and down the trail toward the guard quarters.

Andrij chuckled watching him go. Valentyn would always be a grouch, but his frustration had a tender layer beneath it. It took work to reach that part of him, and jokes and eccentric behavior were not helpful—something Mykyta had yet to figure out after two years in Kynnytsia. Andrij doubted he ever would.

As Andrij led Oleh down the trail behind Valentyn, Mykyta rambled about the gossip of the village. On a normal day, Andrij may have bothered to listen, but between his exhaustion and the journey they faced, who was kissing who was the least of his concerns.

They tied off their horses outside the guard quarters and wandered into the cramped room.

Twenty beds, bunked to maximize usage of the space, lined the walls. A musty smell wafted through the air as Andrij grabbed his gear. It wasn't much—his spear and shield, a canteen, wash kit, iron pot, hatchet, and his furs—but it would be the difference between life and death in the wilds. Boz had sent him on journeys to nearby villages before. This, though, was far further, and he did not want Valentyn mocking him for forgetting the essentials.

As they finished, Mykyta tossed him a hunk of bread. "Doubt you've eaten, so you can take some of mine. Can't have you collapsing on us, can we?"

Andrij devoured it in seconds, yet his hunger wasn't satisfied. Though Valentyn was retrieving the food for the trip, he knew meals on the trail would be even lighter than the measly rations Boz let the guards have. Most warriors had farms of their own around the city, but all twenty of the king's guard had been taken from other villages. They were at his mercy.

"Ready?" Mykyta asked, throwing his bag over his shoulder and smiling boyishly.

Andrij swallowed but nodded. "This isn't how I thought today would go, but I guess we don't have much of a choice?"

Mykyta chuckled. "Do we ever? C'mon. We can't let Valentyn eat all the food before we get there!"

He ran out of the quarters, but Andrij lagged, taking in one last look of the place that had been his home for five years. It was stupid to miss it after Boz had forced him to join the guard. He knew that. Still, a longing gripped his heart—a longing for home, both this one and the one that he'd left so long ago. *Soon…*

But he'd waited long enough. So, after running his fingers across his bed and whispering a prayer to Perun and Jaryło, he stepped into the winter day.

3

GODS, SPRING CANNOT COME SOON ENOUGH.

Andrij winced as he swiped at his frozen brow. Gusts of snow blurred his vision as he rode behind Valentyn, barely able to see his mentor mere strides ahead. The blizzard had caught them by surprise on the second day of their journey. They were nearing the Wyzra River and had intended to cross it before nightfall, but the storm had slowed their trot to a slow walk.

"How far until the Wyzra?" Andrij shouted into the winds.

Valentyn glanced over his shoulder, his beard more white than brown. "You'll know when ya start sinkin'!"

That's reassuring.

Andrij's teeth chattered as his fingers froze against the reins. In his life on the farm, he had spent plenty of nights outside in the frigid winter, but this storm had him in a shock. Neither his furs nor his woolen cloak fended off the gales. Even blinking hurt his face. Still, Oleh pushed on.

"Good boy," Andrij mumbled, leaning into his neck. Blizzard or not, Oleh felt like a furnace beneath the thin pad between him and the horse. That warmth was the only thing keeping his consciousness from slipping away.

Somewhere behind, Kazymyr huffed and whined, but Andrij lacked the energy to look. Mykyta could handle him. He may have been obnoxious, but Mykyta was among the best riders in the guard.

Then someone screamed.

Andrij spun Oleh, sliding his spear from his back as he stared into the sea of snow. "Mykyta?" he asked. "Mykyta!"

No answer came.

Valentyn pulled alongside him with a sigh. "He can't even deal with a bit o' snow?"

Without a reply, Andrij pushed Oleh toward the sound. He couldn't feel his spear's wooden shaft in his numb hand, but he had to be ready to fight. Mykyta rarely went down, and he *never* fell quiet.

The woods revealed nothing. Between the snow and setting sun, the ground was barely visible, let alone the wide area Mykyta could have traveled through the trees. Only hoofprints and the occasional paw marked the snow, and even the places they'd traversed minutes before were covered in a fresh layer of white.

"Where did he go?" Andrij asked himself before shouting for Mykyta again. His voice was just drowned by the storm. There was no sign of either rider or mount anywhere, and when he turned to find Valentyn again, his mentor was gone.

Not good…

Pushing Oleh into a trot, he rushed back toward where he'd seen Valentyn last. The old warrior and Viktor were slower, especially with the snow, but Andrij found only their tracks when he returned. He followed them west, toward the setting sun, and down a slope that forced Oleh to slow. Each step was unsteady, threatening to send them both into the snow—a death sentence in the winter darkness.

"Valentyn!" he called. "Mykyta!"

A gust sent a shiver down Andrij's spine, and he groaned as he wrapped his furs tighter. It was no use. They needed to make camp. They needed to rest, eat, and find warmth around a fire.

Instead, they were wandering without direction, looking for a foolish guard who was probably playing a cruel joke.

Then, as the ground leveled and Dadźbóg's light dipped beneath the horizon, another cry pierced the air.

"Go!" Andrij ordered Oleh, pushing him into a canter. His heart hammered his chest, but he focused only on the source of the noise ahead.

Three figures appeared. One writhed on the ground as the others clashed amid a growing pool of blood.

"Valentyn!" Andrij shouted as his mentor reeled back with ax and shield ready, staring down a dark creature. Black liquid spewed from the holes where its eyes should have been, and its entire human-like body was covered in decaying flesh.

Demon...

"Flank it!" Valentyn ordered.

Andrij glanced at Mykyta, who whimpered in a patch of red snow. "What about Mykyta?"

"Survive first!"

The demon hissed and attacked. It was faster than anything Andrij had seen, and before Valentyn could shout again, it crashed into his shield, slashing his arms with its claws. That spurred Andrij on. He swept around to the demon's right and readied his spear. *Here goes nothing.*

"Now, Andrij!"

He charged as the demon slammed Valentyn down and bit at his neck, only held back by Valentyn's large shield. It snarled, but Andrij's mentor was strong. With a mighty shout, he threw the beast off him—right into Oleh's path.

Andrij grinned as he drove his spear through its chest at full gallop. The demon shrieked but did not fall, and horror swept through Andrij as it rushed after him. He swore under his breath. Despite Oleh's speed, it followed close behind. The only weapons he had left were a hatchet and hunting knife.

It's nothing more than a beast, he told himself. *You've hunted wolf and bear. A demon is no threat.*

Sending Oleh on, he leaped to the ground and crouched behind his shield. Valentyn had struggled against the demon, but if he could hold it long enough for his mentor to join him, it would be two against one. He liked those odds.

The demon lunged as Andrij slid his hunting blade free. A crack tore through the air and his arm ached, but he held against its weight. All his training rushed through his mind as they fought.

When the demon spun and struck, he dodged and kept his shield between them. His knife was too short to reach the beast's head, but it was enough to damage its forearms, making it screech each time it dared to get close.

Come on Valentyn!

Backing down another slope, Andrij gulped down every breath. He'd skirmished against bandits and animals, but this demon was unlike any of them. It never slowed, even with a spear sticking through its sternum. His only chance was to stab it in the head. But how?

The demon charged again, forcing Andrij further down the steepening hill. His feet slipped in the snow as the demon pushed and slashed.

He tumbled.

Andrij's shield slid from his grasp. When he finally stopped rolling, shaking and covered in snow, his skull struck a hard surface. He cried out and gripped his knife with both hands. The creature was only strides away, and he could sense its hunger to kill.

Andrij staggered to his feet. His head throbbed from the impact. With the winds blurring his vision, the world spun around him. He wobbled and collapsed, slamming to the ground again. The snow wasn't enough cushion to stifle the blow, and he groaned, watching the demon sprint to the bottom of the slope just as the earth began to shake.

Andrij scrambled away as fissures split the ground ahead. *Ice! This is the Wyzra!*

The demon hissed and followed, but its steps broke the ice further. As it neared Andrij, a *snap* split the air. The demon's leg slipped into the frigid water. It screamed, and Andrij took advantage of the hesitation, driving his knife into the demon's head and ripping his spear free.

His breath caught as he staggered back and examined the dead creature before him. The ice continued to break at the swift motion. So, slowly, Andrij shuffled toward the other bank, his face stinging and heart racing. He was so close.

Get to the shore, he told himself. *Then you can find Valentyn and Mykyta.* Once Andrij was reunited with the others, would find Oleh and thank the horse for keeping him alive. But as he neared the river's edge, his foot dropped through the ice.

Water swept into his boot, and Andrij winced as he pulled his ankle free and jumped to the river's western bank. He wished for the numbness to return. His entire leg burned worse than his already frozen face. Fire was his only hope, but with his companions and his gear across the river, starting one would be a slow process.

He groaned and glanced across the river. The blizzard blocked his view of the demon, but he knew it was out there. The priests had told tales of their many types—from ovinniks in threshing houses to zmory that sat upon sleeping people and sapped their life—but zmory were undead women, not men. Whatever that thing had been, it was either unheard of or too frightening for the priests to speak of.

Thinking about demons wouldn't save him from the cold. Andrij rose and started gathering whatever kindling he could as he made his way up to the ridge above the river. By the time he arrived, he'd collected enough to attempt a small fire, but with the wind and the dampness of the sticks, it refused to light.

"Swaróg, gift me fire," he prayed.

With a sharp breath, he struck his iron dagger against a stone, once again showering sparks over the tinder in hopes of flame. None came. And as Andrij stood, the gales blew across the sticks, scattering many of them across the ridge.

His heart sank. He cursed Marzanna for her winter, the god Strzybóg for his brutal winds, and

Swaróg for abandoning him. They had only set forth two days before, yet he'd already lost his companions. He would die without fire, without help. Here, west of the Wyzra, Andrij knelt in Krowikie lands. It was the furthest he had ever gone, and already, he wished to turn back.

"Why does it have to be me?" he asked the storm. "Why must my tribe depend on me?"

The kindling erupted, sending a wave of heat crashing over him. He spun away and reached for his shield in expectation of another attack, but a bright bird dove through the storm and into the fire. Though set ablaze, it was not consumed. Instead, its power seemed to swell, and the Firebird emerged from the flames in a brilliant light that burned away the blizzard.

Andrij covered his eyes as they watered. "Firebird! Firebird! What have I done to earn your presence?" There were as many legends of the Firebird as those of the witch of the Mangled Woods and the gods themselves. Until now, Andrij had believed them to be just that—legends.

"Look upon me, traveler, and hear the truth," a strong woman's voice said.

He did, and awe filled him as he watched the flames, crowning the bird in a golden glory. *What more is this journey if the Firebird would come to me?*

"Marzanna's wrath should have taken you this eve," the voice continued. "Though you saved one of your companions from her nezhit, you would have frozen on this ridge had I not called upon this Firebird."

Bowing his head, Andrij took a sharp breath. "You're a goddess! Who else could control the Firebird?"

"Yes, Andrij. I am called Dziewanna, queen of the wilds. You and your people have foolishly forgotten me, but *I* have saved you from Marzanna." The Firebird slashed its wings through the air at the mention of her name. "My sister seeks to separate the tribes, to make you weak. If she succeeds, then all of Jawia is destined for years of winter—of starvation and death."

"How?" Andrij shook his head. "The equinox is days away! Jaryło will kill her, right?"

The goddess sighed. "Marzanna's spite cannot be quelled so easily. Jaryło and I have fought to keep our sister in check for centuries, but there is something far greater than us at work. Though I will do what I must, I fear it may not be enough."

The Firebird dropped, landing in the melted snow before Andrij. Its flames snapped and flickered around it, and as Dziewanna continued, Andrij felt her rage, "She has stolen everything from us, betrayed us! Her desire for death and suffering is too great to continue beyond the winter moons, and I *will* burn her to ash when the time comes. But without the tribes' sacrifices, without their strength, I cannot end her. You must complete your journey."

"My goddess, how does my journey help stop Marzanna? I am to ask the Krowikie to fight the clans of the east, nothing more."

"It is not what you will do but what you will send into motion." The Firebird drew closer, its heat singing Andrij's skin. "I cannot know what is ahead. None know Destiny's will, not even the gods. I believe, though, there lies a pair in Dwie Rzeki who can change the fate of Jawia, of the world. Your message will bring about their own journey—one more difficult than any mortal has ever known."

Change the fate of Jawia? "Who? How will I know where to find them?"

"You will not. Someday, you may meet if they survive their trials, but before then, you will face many struggles of your own." The flames dimmed slightly, and the bird hung its head. "It is still Marzanna's time. Though my strength is fading, the blizzard has all but passed. One of your companions has fallen to my sister, but the other is coming here now with the horse you call Oleh. Go, ride through the night, and do not rest when the godless moon shows its face."

"Wait!" Andrij shouted, but the Firebird took flight in a rush and soared into the night, its flames following it until the bird appeared as another flickering soul in the sky. Behind remained only a single feather, still ablaze. He took it in his hand, yet it did not hurt as the fire danced through his fingers. *What is this?*

As Andrij looked to where the Firebird had flown, he thanked the goddess for his second chance at life. It was a gift he would cherish. Though her warning overwhelmed his mind, Dziewanna had saved him for a single purpose— to finish his journey. And finish it he would. Whether through storm or against demons, he would fight on, for his tribe, for his family, and for the goddess who had placed her faith in him.

4

"SHE SAID WHAT NOW?**" V**ALENTYN GROANED as he rubbed his thighs. "Better be good to keep me ridin' so long."

Darkness swallowed the world as their exhausted horses carried them through the woods west of the Wyzra. Despite Valentyn's assurances that crossing the river would be the hardest part of the trip, Andrij dreaded the days ahead. If the goddess of winter truly was trying to stop them, then what else lay ahead? The creature had killed Mykyta, who, according to Valentyn, had bled out until he burst into flames, allowing his soul to travel to the underworld of Nawia. That loss weighed on him. Friend or not, Mykyta had been a companion, and Andrij missed his ramblings already.

Sighing, Andrij buried his thoughts before describing his encounter with the Firebird again. Like most of the guards, Valentyn was skeptical of tales like this, but he was Astiwie. Most within the tribe understood there were powers far beyond what they could grasp.

"Explains Mykyta's fire," Valentyn said before shaking his head. "Kid was too young. They're always too young..."

Andrij raised his brow. "You don't seem surprised by the Firebird."

Valentyn shrugged. "Listen, if you get to be as old as me as a guard, you've seen more than you're willing to admit. Usually its 'cause of too many swigs of oskoła, but if you swear you saw it, I ain't one to doubt it. Doesn't change much anyway. We're going to Dwie Rzeki whether this *Dziewanna* wants us to or not."

"But what about the pair in the village or Marzanna's plan? That doesn't scare you? Mykyta died so fast. We could be next."

"I'll die when it's my time. Besides, Mykyta will be enjoying the paradise of Nawia while we're still obeying king lunatic's orders. Ever thought ya might be better off in Mykyta's spot?"

With a tight grip on his reins, Andrij considered that for a moment before forcing away the temptation. "No. My family needs me."

"Your family probably thinks you're dead, kid. Boz pulls boys like you out of random farms *because* so many of his guards die following his whims. They wouldn't know the difference if you'd froze last night."

"You're wrong!" Andrij spun Oleh around to block Viktor and his mentor. Their gazes met, and for once, Valentyn backed down. "My mother said she'd wait for my return, and I will go to here when we're finished. Boz has promised my freedom."

A shadow fell over Valentyn's rugged face. "I had your fight once. Goes faster than ya think." He rounded Andrij and continued through the trees, his gaze focused on something immaterial.

Groaning, Andrij followed. Pain and regret or not, he had a job to do. It didn't matter that Boz was the one forcing him west. Between the Horde the clan riders had spoken of and Dziewanna's warnings, there was something much larger at play. If either were true, he had to finish the journey. For both his tribe and his family, he would reach Dwie Rzeki and bring his king an army. He would be a hero. More importantly, he'd be free.

They trekked through the night in silence, only the sound of the barbarous northern wind tearing through the trees to keep them company. Valentyn's cape—blue and gold like Boz's—

drifted through the little moonlight as he rode. Andrij studied the Astiwie symbol of the kalina plant embroidered upon it: red berries for blood and white flowers for purity. *One out of two at least...*

"Why do you think Boz kept the kalina?" Andrij asked, pulling alongside Valentyn. "He hated his family."

Valentyn considered that for a second. "The little I know about power tells me one thing."

"What's that?"

He chuckled. "No one cares what you think, just what you do for 'em. Before King Boz, bandits raided the outer villages all the time, but, crazy as he may be, Boz found all of them. Cut off enough heads and men stop thinking a raid is worth it."

"What about the ovinniks, the grain shortages?"

"You know our people."

Andrij nodded. "Blame the weather and demons and they'll believe it, but we *know* how to tame some of them. At least the priests claim so."

"You're from a small village, kid. Think about it. You ever see a priest who knew anything before Kynnytsia?"

"Fair point." Khakovo's bumbling idiot of a priest had barely remembered the names of the gods when he was sober, which was rare. The priests of Kynnytsia had their own intentions. Everyone knew that. But at least they pretended to care about what they preached.

When daylight cracked above the horizon, Andrij smiled at the thought of sleep. His soreness from their battle with the nezhit had long numbed, but his eyes slipped shut every few seconds, demanding rest.

They stopped beneath an elm, its wide, strong branches offering some shadows as they lay on their bed rolls and wrapped themselves in their furs. He'd awaited this moment for hours, and as the sun climbed above the trees, he took one long breath before fading to sleep.

"Andrij."

Andrij winced as he opened his eyes, the sunlight splitting the gaps of the naked branches. His arms ached and his head throbbed from its impact against the ice. By Dadźbóg's position, it was just past noon, but his mentor hovered over him, breaking the rays as he shook Andrij.

"Andrij, get up!"

Pushing away his dreariness, Andrij scanned his surroundings. "What's wrong?"

Then he heard the *snap* from the woods. He was on his feet in an instant with both spear and shield in hand, his breaths controlled and his mind ready for a fight. Valentyn took his side, gripping his ax. "Someone's watchin' us. Could feel it last night."

"And you didn't say anything?"

"You spook easy. Needed you rested."

Andrij huffed. "Well, I'm rested now. Where's the stalker?"

Valentyn nodded to a thicket twenty-strides north, down the slope to the Wyzra. Whoever it was, they had the high ground. "C'mon. Let's smoke the scoundrel."

They crept forward with their shields locked. Two wasn't enough for a shield wall, but it created a solid enough front to hold back a frontal attack, and the symbols of Perun's Thundermark painted on them would scare away minor demons. At least, that's what the priests claimed.

A gust swept through the woods, stinging Andrij's face as they approached the thicket, but he ignored the pain. Mykyta was dead because they'd been too slow to stop the nezhit. This time, his training would not fail him. Valentyn had been by his side since the moment he stepped into Kynnytsia, and he wouldn't lose his mentor now—not to demon, animal, or man.

The thicket stirred as Andrij yelled and drove his spear into its branches, finding nothing but wood. Again he struck, and again the dense brush rejected his attempt. Crouching, he examined the maze of thorns and vines. "It's empty, Valentyn."

"It's not!" Valentyn pushed him aside and swung his ax into the branches. Thorns jabbed at his arms, but he pushed on until Andrij grabbed his tunic.

"Valentyn! It's empty!"

The old warrior stopped. With hearty breaths, he examined the scrapes in his tunic and his blood dripping to the snow. "Ay… Seems I got a lil' carried away."

Andrij chuckled and patted Valentyn's shoulder. "We're both shaken up after yesterday, but nothing's following us." He glanced at the sun as it began its descent. "It's about time we left, though. You sure you're ready to ride?"

"Am I sure I'm ready? Pah!" Valentyn stomped past him and began packing his gear onto Viktor, who was tied to a tree not far away. "I've seen more than my share of death. Pray to the gods you never have to remember the faces I do."

For a moment, Andrij watched Valentyn with worry. There was no doubt he'd lost more than Mykyta, but Valentyn had never lost his temper so quickly before—at least, not around Andrij. Whether it was the nezhit's attack or something else, something had him anxious.

"C'mon, boy!" Valentyn said. "Boz ain't a patient man, and I've heard enough stories to know Jacek's the same."

Andrij mounted Oleh and slipped a spare bit of grain to the horse, who huffed happily at the offering. "You just want to arrive in time for the Drowning of Marzanna rituals," Andrij laughed.

Valentyn grinned and shook the layer of white from his beard. "Not the ritual but the oskoła. The Krowikie have enough of it to make any warrior fall flat on his face in glee—and that's before ya see the women." He chuckled. "Oh, that got your attention."

"I'm not *that* desperate." Andrij averted his gaze, thinking of the many girls who'd denied his advances and the two who'd ducked into the woods with him more than once. Even those dalliances had ended as quickly as they had begun, though.

"Ya don't need to be desperate to want these ones."

Andrij shook his head as they continued their journey west. "I'll just take your word for it."

5

After another night of riding through the darkness, Andrij came to an uncomfortable conclusion: They were in fact being followed.

Valentyn claimed they were nearing a village that would hold both supplies and better places to sleep than the ground, but as Dadźbóg flickered behind the blanket of clouds above, Andrij doubted his mentor's memory. They had passed a few villages in recent days. None, though, were any larger than the tiny one of three families that Andrij had grown up in himself. The people needed the little food they had this late in winter, and there were no signs of a larger settlement. Surely a hunting party would have left some tracks nearby if Valentyn had been right?

In fact, the only tracks they had seen were those of a solitary wolf. It kept its distance, ahead at times and behind at others, but Andrij spotted its prints in the soft snow as they trotted.

Why would a wolf stalk us?

That question haunted him. Wolves were dangerous in packs, but alone, they were hardly a threat against two armed warriors. If it was following them, there had to be another reason.

"Marzanna…"

Her name chilled his tongue as he spoke. Dziewanna had warned him of the winter goddess. Could this be one of her servants, or was he mistaking a lone, possibly starving, wolf for something much bigger? He didn't know, but it was indeed watching them. He was certain of that.

"Don't go praying to her now," Valentyn muttered. "Jaryło will slay her in days."

Andrij pushed Oleh up beside Valentyn and Viktor. Despite being nearly a head taller than Valentyn on foot, their eyes were level due to Viktor's ridiculous height. There was no reason for Valentyn to ride such a ginormous horse—except for his ego.

"Gods, I'd never pray to her," Andrij replied. "I noticed wolf tracks a while back, and I think you're right. Marzanna sent a wolf to stalk us."

Valentyn smiled proudly, revealing the two teeth missing on his right side. "Say it again."

"What?"

"I'm right! Ha!"

Andrij rolled his eyes. "Aren't you worried a wolf is following us?"

Valentyn patted the ax at his side. "Ain't nothing to worry about. I saw his eyes in the dark—big and blue those ones—but I've fought plenty of wolves. I got a feeling he's just watching."

"For now…"

Valentyn huffed and pushed Viktor into a canter that the horse resisted for as long as possible. As Andrij followed, the old warrior called back, "Maybe you do need one of those Dwie Rzeki girls to loosen you up." He chuckled. "Village shouldn't be too far. Małe Wzgórze I think it was called."

" 'Little Hill'? I don't see any—" He stopped as a trail appeared before them, sloping upward. "—hill," he finished.

"Told ya to trust me," Valentyn said. "In a few minutes, we'll be filling our bellies and—"

A shout cut him off as a boy, no taller than Andrij's hip, ran from the brush with a bent spear in hand. Andrij smiled at its sloppily carved tip. *Someone's too young for iron.*

"Raiders!" the boy shouted, skidding to a stop three strides away and realizing he was obviously overmatched. "The raiders are back!"

The riders swapped glances as a woman led a group of men down the trail with various hasty weapons in hand: hatchets, hoes, and sickles. They approached as one grabbed the child, scolding him as he did.

These men aren't warriors. Their chief had likely left for Dwie Rzeki with his best men and eligible girls. The festival honored both the coming of spring equinox and sixteen-year-olds as adults, eligible to be wed. Only the older men remained.

"You are mistaken," Andrij began, clearing his throat and trying to sound as confident as possible. "We are not raiders. I am Andrij Myroslavovych Ya—"

"No one cares about your name," the woman interrupted. She stepped forward, her hair wrapped beneath a flimsy woolen cap and her brown dress torn in multiple places. "We've got nothing left to give. Especially not to you Astiwie."

Andrij sighed. *Is it common for Krowikie women to lead?* "We seek nothing but a warm bed for the night as allies of your high chief. We come under the orders of King Boz Vladyslavovych Kramarenko."

The woman gripped her sickle and furrowed her brow. "You don't get it. Raiders have taken everything from us. They'll come back tonight to steal whatever's left. You don't want to be here, and we don't want you here."

"And High Chief Jacek won't send men to help you?"

"Our lands are not like yours, Astiwie. The high chief barely controls the most influential chiefs, let alone villages like ours. He may claim to rule us, but he has neither the men nor the will to protect our village."

Valentyn eyed Andrij. "Don't do it," he whispered.

But as Andrij sat tall and looked down at the woman, memories of fields ablaze met him.

He had been eleven, less than a year before he would complete his hunt and earn his first haircut—the first step toward manhood. From then on, his father would train him to follow in his footsteps. For Andrij, though, that day would never come.

The raiders came without warning. As Khakovo had no warriors or real weapons, those who bothered to put up a real fight were slaughtered. Andrij's eldest brother, Drugov, was among them, and he wept alongside his family for days as their farm burned. What little jewelry his mother had was taken along with much of their grain and his father's favored cattle. They'd never been rich, but now, they had nothing. It was in the aftermath of the raid that Andrij's father went to King Boz for the resources to plant a new crop and breed new livestock.

Unfortunately, the king's demands were steep, so Andrij's family worked for moons in order to repay Boz's claimed 'generosity.' Then the raiders returned.

After slaying Andrij's father, they stole what remained of the king's resources. When Boz's men showed up a year later to collect their king's due, he found a family of little more than beggars, scrounging what little they could from their burned land just to survive.

They took Andrij instead.

Now, Andrij's breaths caught as he looked from the woman to the quivering boy, barely younger than he'd been. Five years before, he'd been unable to protect his family. King Boz had forced him into his service because of those raiders, taken him from his family. Maybe

Valentyn had been right. They could've forgotten him after all these years, or they could've starved with nothing. If Andrij had a chance to save these people from that same fate, though, he had to take it.

"We will help you stop their attack if you allow us to rest here tonight," he finally said. Andrij's nerves drifted away as he spoke, and he puffed up his chest with a warrior's strength. "How many men are in their band?"

Valentyn shook his head as the woman stared at Andrij, eyes wide. "Twenty," she said, "maybe more, all with spears and shields."

"We're doomed, kid," Valentyn muttered. "Best to ride west while we can."

Ignoring his mentor, Andrij scanned the crowd. "And are these all your people who remain?" He counted eleven. Not enough. Though he and Valentyn were trained—and Valentyn had retrieved Andrij's shield from the Wyzra's bank—numbers were crucial in such a fight.

She nodded. "All the men."

"Very well," Andrij continued, dismounting and striding to the woman. "We will need your women to stand with us then."

"I don't—"

"Listen to the boy," Valentyn said, still on Viktor's back. "I don't want to be here, but he does. If ya don't do this his way, then you're on your own."

Andrij stopped before the woman. "What's your name?"

Meeting his gaze, she crossed her arms. "Beáta."

"Beáta," he said with a nod, "you are bold to lead in the absence of your chief. We can help you get rid of these raiders, but we need *all* of your people to help if we are to protect your village."

Beáta stepped back. Her eyes were stern, but she waved for them to follow. "Come."

The gathered people walked alongside Andrij and Valentyn as they climbed the hill toward the Małe Wzgórze village center. Andrij felt their stares, heavy upon him like an ox's yoke. In a moment, he had taken their safety as his own responsibility. If only he knew how he'd protect them.

As they walked, Beáta explained more about the raiders, who were led by a man she called Ctirad. They had waited until the village chief had left with the few men trained with a spear.

The destruction they'd wrought became obvious at the village center. Cottage doors were smashed in, and corpses of both sheep and goats lay rotting in snowed pastures. A putrid smell struck Andrij's nose as he passed the well before the chief's longhouse. When he looked down it, he gagged and stumbled back.

Valentyn raised his brow. "What spooked ya?"

"There's a body in the well," Andrij mumbled, shaking his head to get the image out of his head.

Beáta nodded, the dark rings beneath her eyes now apparent in the clearing. "Radoš was his name. He'll turn to a demon if we can't burn the body. I figure the raiders threw him in there to keep us away from the well."

"Crude but effective," Valentyn replied. "Why haven't ya taken him out?"

"They took our rope, mister!" the boy with the spear exclaimed. "Pa had a good stretch of it before…"

Beáta stroked the boy's hair before ushering for him to join a man and woman Andrij assumed to be his parents. "They stole most of our tools, livestock, and what little valuables we had," she said. "Tonight, Ctirad claimed he would take what remained of our food. Not that we have much to give."

With a glance in Andrij's direction, Valentyn handed Viktor's reins to him before pulling a short coil of rope from his pack. " 'Never travel without a rope,' my father always said. Ironic that it killed 'im in the end."

"Lower me down," Andrij said. "I'll grab the body while you pull."

Valentyn huffed, pushing him aside. "I'm lighter. Would hate for ya to have to swim with a corpse. If someone's got to pull it up, might as well be me." His gaze drifted to Beáta as he removed his pack and Astiwie cloak, handing the latter to Andrij with a reverence Andrij didn't know his mentor possessed.

Is he fond of this woman?

The weight of the battle ahead had Andrij's nerves frayed, but Valentyn held his chin high. The old warrior's resistance to helping Małe Wzgórze seemed to have faded too. If Beáta was the reason why, then Andrij thanked the gods for Valentyn's unending desire to find a woman.

Rope tied tight around his waist, Valentyn put one foot on the well as Andrij and a few other men grabbed the free end. "Don't drop me, or you'll regret it!"

"I'd rather not have you coming back to haunt me," Andrij replied, unable to chuckle at the joke.

Every time he looked at the destroyed village, a longing for home throbbed in his chest.

Valentyn dropped without warning.

The rope pulled taught, and Andrij gritted his teeth as it tore at his palms. Why had Valentyn jumped so quickly? It couldn't be just to impress Beáta. Valentyn took risks at times, yes, but he wasn't *that* vain.

After a minute of silence and worried glances, a tug finally came on the rope. "Oi! Pull me up before I drown down here why don't ya!"

Relief washed over Andrij, and this time, he allowed himself to smile as they pulled Valentyn back up. Soon, Valentyn appeared with a sopping wet corpse in his arms. He shivered as he met the cold breeze, but Andrij knew his mentor wouldn't show his pain. Especially with Beáta watching.

"Not a problem at all," Valentyn said as he set down the body and held his hands at his hips. "Best to burn the body soon. That stench ought to kill us all otherwise."

A group rushed to him, offering their thanks, before they wept over the body. *Just like Drugov.* Andrij fought tears at the memory of his brother run through by a raider's spear. These people deserved their chance to mourn and ensure this man could enter Nawia's paradise, not be trapped as some demon in the well.

Andrij offered Valentyn his cloak before winding the rope. Using his hands made him feel useful, despite his uncertainty of defying the raiders. "We should probably get you some new clothes if you don't want to freeze to death."

"I'll be fine," Valentyn said as Beáta approached and bowed.

"We owe you a great debt," she said. "The least of which can be repaid with a new tunic and trousers." Valentyn opened his mouth to object, but she wagged a finger. "I won't be hearing any complaints from you. I am our village's healer, and I cannot have you running amok in wet clothes when Marzanna's Curse could befall you. Come."

Andrij chuckled as she dragged away Valentyn. "While you're away, I will begin training the people for battle."

Valentyn's only reply was a grunt before he disappeared into Beáta's cottage.

6

THIS WON'T END WELL.

Andrij watched the gathered men and women swing their make-shift weapons as Valentyn instructed them. His mentor had emerged from Beáta's cottage much happier than when he'd entered, but both of their moods had soured since then. There were only twenty-four villagers capable of holding a spear, plus the two Astiwie. Without training or shields, it wouldn't be enough.

The small farms scattered across Małe Wzgórze wouldn't provide much cover either. Even with the chief and a few more warriors, defending the village would be difficult without a wall. They needed experienced fighters, not farmers and their wives.

Andrij reached into his bag and felt the Firebird's feather, still ablaze. Dziewanna had saved him once. She could offer these people hope, but this wasn't Marzanna's demon. Andrij had been the one to volunteer to stop the raiders, so he would stop the raiders… somehow.

The sunlight waned as Valentyn shuffled over, stroking his beard. "They're hopeless, but you're right, that's exactly why they need us."

Andrij nodded. "If we're to ask for the high chief's aid, the least we can do is help protect his villages. Besides, my home was just like this one. I can't just let them lose everything knowing I could have helped them stand against these raiders."

"You'll be the death of me, kid." Valentyn took a deep sigh and looked to the setting sun. "But it's been a long time since I've done something that feels right. Da, maybe this is it."

Without a reply, Andrij patted him on the shoulder and paced before the gathered crowd. Men frowned, women trembled, and boys too young to see battle smirked, not knowing what horrors they were about to face. *These people would've lived if I hadn't spoken. Their possessions may have been stolen and their farms ravaged, but they would've lived.*

He shook his head. No, that wasn't living. It was torture, clinging to survival and devouring every last scrap you could without knowing whether it would be your last. He'd felt that hunger, that pain. It had grown with each passing day until desperation warped his mind. Andrij wasn't proud of his thoughts during that time. The things he'd considered...

Swallowing, he straightened his posture and forced himself to look like the general the village needed. "These raiders have taken all you have while your chief drinks in Dwie Rzeki. But that ends tonight." Holding up the flaming feather, he continued. "A Firebird sent by the goddess Dziewanna has blessed our mission west, and that means she's protecting all of us. Let her fury burn all who threaten this village!"

Andrij stopped before a couple, clutching each other's hands as the rest of the crowd shouted in support. There was fear in their eyes.

"By standing up to these raiders, you are far braver than most," he said to them. "I can't promise anything, but we'll do all we can to protect your village." If only he knew how.

The flames danced around his hand as he paced away, examining the clearing that made the village center. Outnumbered and with inferior training and weapons, they had little hope without a trick. He held up the feather. *Maybe Dziewanna knew this would happen.*

He spun and pointed to Beáta. "Do you have oskoła, any alcohol or oils?"

"Yes, but—"

"Get it," Andrij interrupted. "We can burn them if we act quickly. Bring all of it the village has and spread it out around the trailheads."

Beáta scampered off, grabbing a few of the men as she did. *This better work*, Andrij thought as he clutched the feather. The fire wouldn't kill all the raiders, but it would give them a chance. That was enough.

"I don't know if I should be angry or proud," Valentyn said, stepping to his side.

"Sorry. It was the oskoła or our lives." Andrij patted him on the back. "But if we make it to Dwie Rzeki, you said there would be more, right?"

"There better be."

The men emerged from their cottages with buckets of oskoła, and Andrij directed them where to pour it. Soon, the liquid trickled down the trails and covered the furthest section of the village center, away from the buildings.

Andrij grinned as they finished, gathering around him. "Allow them to enter until they reach the end of the wet patch. I will stand with Beáta as the rest of you hide out in the woods.

Wait for the fire to ignite, and then attack in the chaos that follows." He scanned the crowd. "Any questions?"

No one stirred. *Hopefully that's a good sign.*

"All right, then. Move into positions. Dadźbóg's light will be gone soon."

The crowd scattered, and Valentyn nodded to him one last time. "Stay alive. There's too many women in Dwie Rzeki for just me to handle."

Andrij grabbed his mentor's forearm. "Even if we survive this, women are the least of my concern."

With a hearty chuckle, Valentyn jogged into the wood, and Andrij hoped that wouldn't be the last time he saw him. There was no time for pondering, though. The sun would set in minutes, and he needed to be prepared when the raiders arrived.

Beáta took a shaky breath as she joined Andrij. "You think it'll work?"

"No idea."

She raised her brow. "Then why tell them this goddess you call Dziewanna will aid us? No mere torch would ignite the oskoła with it soaking into the snow. Either the goddess saves us or we're dead."

As the light disappeared, Andrij held up the Firebird's feather, flickering in the darkness. "Then let us pray she hears our call."

Torchlight appeared at the base of the hill, and Andrij slid the feather up his sleeve. *You can do this.* He'd never led people before, let alone those fighting for their own village. Each of their lives weighed on his shoulders as the raiders neared, their torches illuminating their grimy faces and cracked shields. In the darkness, there could've been fifteen or fifty. Andrij just hoped Beáta's count had been close. If there were more raiders than she'd expected, it would be a massacre.

"Beáta!" the lead raider shouted, opening his arms with shield and spear still in hand. Black paint ran from his forehead to his full cheeks, and torn leather armor covered his round body.

"Ctirad, welcome," Beáta replied, bowing her head.

Andrij remained standing. "There is nothing left for you to take."

Ctirad smirked and swung his spear, bringing its tip only inches from Andrij's nose. "There is always more."

"But you can't have it." Andrij slid the feather from his sleeve, dropping it upon the oskoła at

Ctirad's feet and praying silently that Dziewanna aided them.

Shock filled the raiders' eyes, but they were too slow. The fire swallowed them in an instant, racing through the village center and slicing down the trails. Screams filled the air. Then came the yells of the villagers.

The smell of burning flesh stung Andrij's nose as Ctirad dove from the flames, still ablaze and swatting at his seared armor. He found no aid.

Beáta swung her sickle into the raider's neck as Andrij grabbed the Firebird feather. Ctirad's body slumped to the ground, but Beáta sliced again and again. Andrij looked away as she decapitated the man in her fury.

When Beáta yelled and raised her weapon, Andrij met her gaze. He winced at the blood strewn across her face. "We have to help the others," she said, her voice stern.

They charged into the fray. Many of the raiders had fallen in the flames, but a dozen remained, cutting down women, men, and children alike as they rushed up the hill. Andrij couldn't tell how many villagers had been slain. It didn't matter. One was too many to lose to these brutes, and he would make them pay.

Andrij's spear found the first raider's stomach with little effort, slipping by his damaged shield. A second shouted from his flank as he spun. The spear raced toward his stomach, but Andrij knocked aside the weapon and drove his spear into the attacker's thigh. Screaming, the raider dropped to a knee as Andrij drew his hunting knife and sliced his throat without hesitation.

That's two.

Smoke obscured the battle around him. Cries and yells echoed down the hill, but there was little to separate friend from foe. Everywhere Andrij looked, people dropped to the dirt, forever leaving Jawia for a life beyond. Had he failed? And where was Valentyn?

Another raider burst through the smoke with a sword in hand, catching Andrij in his thoughts. He barely raised his shield in time to deflect the raider's first blow, and with his spear still stuck in the downed attacker's thigh, Andrij had nothing but knife and hatchet to fight with—again.

The raider charged him over and over, battering Andrij's shield with every strike and driving him down the slope. Each swing of Andrij's knife met air as his feet slipped in the snow. The battle had lasted only minutes, yet he was exhausted. His eyes stung from the smoke, and each breath ended as a sputter.

Keep fighting, he told himself. *You were trained for this.*

Yet the raider was stronger, better armed. Andrij's shield cracked from the onslaught, and the top third of it gave way as his pursuer slammed his own shield into Andrij's. Andrij swore under his breath and spun away, just avoiding another strike.

Ice cracked beneath his feet. Sweat poured down his face, mixing with blood as the raider forced him closer to the trail's flames. Andrij spat, but the taste of salt and iron lingered. "C'mon! What are you waiting for?"

The raider smiled with his broken teeth and lunged. Andrij waited until the last second before diving to the side, sending the raider onto the ice and then slipping into the fire.

On the ground, the snow burned Andrij's skin, but he laughed as he stood. It had been a silly trick. He was alive, though, and the raider's screams were music to his ears. King Boz would've been proud of him. Was that a good thing?

One last cry tore through the air before silence.

Only the crackle of the slowly dying fires greeted Andrij as he stood, the smoke still obscuring any view of survivors. When he retrieved his spear and trudged to the hill's peak, he saw the villagers' heavy faces. Blood soaked their clothes as they dropped their make-shift weapons and hugged those who remained. They had won, but from Andrij's count, eleven were missing. Valentyn and Beáta were among them.

Andrij turned back toward the battle, waiting for his mentor's stout body to appear. *Come on, Valentyn. Don't leave me now…*

For too long he waited with his pulse hammering his mind. Just as his patience ran out, a cough broke through the smoke as two figures climbed the trail. Valentyn's dark beard was charred at its ends and blood seeped from a wound on his leg, but he fought on with Beáta's arm slung over his shoulder. Together, they limped to the village center, where they dropped to their knees with a collective huff.

Andrij rushed to them. "Thank the gods!"

"Thank Dziewanna," Beáta said, pushing away the stray brown hairs that had fallen into her face. "And thank you, Firebringer."

"Oh, thank *him*!" Valentyn grumbled. "Not like I saved ya from the flames…"

With a wry smile, Beáta rose, holding a hand to Valentyn's cheek for a moment. "Thank you both—and to all of you." She surveyed those who remained. They had lost nearly half of those who had joined the fight, but they had killed every last raider. "Our village has suffered today, but we are free from Ctirad's grasp!"

The villagers nodded in recognition, too weary to give any more. Andrij couldn't blame them. Death was no stranger to the tribes, especially in the harsh winter moons, but to have lost so much of their small settlement in minutes was a blow they would never forget—he never had. There was triumph over the raiders. As Andrij studied the mourning strangers in the dying firelight, though, he wondered if it had been worth the loss.

"Come," Beáta said to him and Valentyn. "You have more than earned a warm home to lay your heads, and I must tend to Valentyn's wound. The blade's slice was deep."

Valentyn once again tried to object, but she shushed him as they hobbled toward her cottage. Andrij followed, stepping into a warm room. The glow of the hearth revealed two doorways, covered with nothing more than sheets of fabric. Beáta brought Valentyn into the one on the right and laid him down on a bed. When Andrij entered, she nodded to the second. "You two may stay here as long as you wish. Because of you, we will not starve, so you may take whatever you need to finish your journey."

Andrij shook his head as she grabbed rags and examined Valentyn's wound. "This is too much. You have little, and we need no more than food for tonight."

"Do not reject our hospitality after what you just did for us," Beáta replied, insistent. "Radogost would not look kindly on us failing to take care of you."

Andrij chuckled at her invocation of the god of hospitality but surrendered to her will. "Very well. Thank you, Beáta."

With a yelp, Valentyn gripped her arm, taking the pressure off his leg. "No more of that!"

She scowled. "If you don't wish to lose your leg, then you'll stop complaining. You, Andrij, take the dagger on the table and heat it in the hearth. There's no time for me to sew such a large wound."

Nodding, Andrij scrambled into the main room and grabbed the iron dagger upon it. To see Valentyn in so distress… He winced. Cauterizing the wound would be no less painful, but if it kept his mentor alive, Andrij would help Beáta do what she needed to.

The flames flickered around the blade for a few minutes as Andrij tapped his foot and looked toward Valentyn. The warrior's groans weren't muffled by the fabric between rooms, and each one gripped Andrij's heart. In had been so long since he'd lost his brother, then his real father. But in the time since, Valentyn had been Andrij's only family. He couldn't lose him now.

When the blade was hot, Andrij rushed back to Beáta and slid the hilt into her hand. She didn't tremble as she held it flat against the wound. She'd already slid a stick into Valentyn's mouth, and it stifled his screams until the gruesome process was finally finished.

Swiftly, she rose and took a deep breath. "My apologies for the pain. This was the only option."

Valentyn's breaths were raspy as he lay on the bed, staring at her with tears in his eyes. "Don't apologize for saving my life. Nawia may be a paradise, but I'd rather stay here, especially if you're around."

Beáta raised her brow. "It will be *you* who is around me for longer. With that leg, you won't be riding anytime soon."

"What?" Andrij exclaimed, gripping his head. "We need to reach Dwie Rzeki by the Drowning of Marzanna. There's no time to wait!"

"What you need to do is irrelevant. Valentyn must rest. Besides, the ride to the capital is no more than three days from here. Nothing a strapping warrior like you can't handle, right?"

I can see why Valentyn likes her. Beáta had a fight in her. No simple woman could handle Valentyn's mood, but around her, Valentyn seemed the weaker of the pair. "It may be possible, but—"

"Go, boy," Valentyn mumbled. His eyes were glazed as he fought to stay awake after losing so much blood. "Enjoy the festival without me. I'll be ready to go when ya return."

Andrij sat on the other bed, staring at the dirt beneath his boots. "Then I'll ride alone."

Anxiety entrapped his chest. His breaths were short as he thought of everything relying on the journey's completion: his freedom, his tribe's hopes against the clans, and potentially even winter's end. Though he still didn't understand why, Dziewanna had sent the Firebird for a reason. Andrij promised himself he wouldn't fail the goddess. He would reach Dwie Rzeki. He would bring the Krowikie army to his tribe's defense. And he would ensure the pair who Dziewanna had spoken of began their own journey—whatever that was.

"Very well," Beáta said with a swift bow of her head. "If you must leave in the morning, I will return soon with food and any supplies we can spare. For tonight, however, you both must rest." Then she stepped through the strip of fabric, leaving behind the smell of lilacs mixed with smoke as Valentyn's snoring filled the room.

7

ANDRIJ ROSE THE NEXT DAY with a full stomach and a rested but sore body. For each moment after, villagers stopped into the cottage to wish both him and Valentyn well, but there was sorrow in their eyes—the same sorrow in Andrij's heart. Like them, he had lost those he loved because of forces outside his control. That longing to be with them lingered wherever he went, but at least he had hope to reunite with his family. The villagers had lost theirs forever.

Once the villagers had finally left, Valentyn huffed and scratched his beard.

"What?" Andrij asked as he prepared his pack.

"Just thinking 'bout the Krowikie."

Andrij smirked. "Please tell me it's something other than their women. After leading a dozen of them into battle, I don't know if I'm more intrigued or frightened."

"I'm capable of other thoughts!" Valentyn exclaimed before glancing at the fabric between the rooms. But Beáta was gone, doing her part to rebuild the village.

"Oh, really? Tell me, then. What was it you were thinking about? Beáta?"

Valentyn ignored the last question and swept his arm toward the door. "The trail west of here. It was here last time I went with Boz, but why don't they build more of them?"

"Huh…" Andrij tried to remember if they had seen any others outside of villages themselves, but he couldn't. "That must make Małe Wzgórze a pretty sizeable village if it's important enough for a trail, but I would hardly consider it *that* large. Boz told me the Krowikie were dispersed. I guess I didn't realize how much."

"The king and the Krowikie ain't good friends," Valentyn replied. "We might be allies, but I doubt he likes to talk about them much. Not that he likes talking to you at all. They're spread out because they were divided between at least fifteen chiefs until twenty-or-so years ago. Jacek united all of them when he defended against Solga's invasion from the west—with Boz's help. Then they made him high chief." He shrugged. "Well, that's what the stories say at least."

"And Jacek can keep them in line without trails to move his warriors?" Andrij shook his head. Boz would be disappointed in his counterpart. When Boz had crowned himself king, he had ordered trails built to connect all the villages in Astiwie lands. Though he still claimed it was for the sake of trade, everyone knew it was to ensure the many warriors in Kynnytsia could march as quickly as possible against bandits or rebels.

Valentyn shrugged. "Men remember what Jacek has done for his people. His villages have enough warriors for him to send against bandits out here, but ya gotta realize the Krowikie fear the Solgawi more than anything."

"Then what hope do we have of him sending his warriors east? If he needs every man he has to defend against a potential Solgawi attack, an invasion three hundred miles away means nothing."

"The last war was bloodier than any for generations." Valentyn rolled up his right sleeve, revealing a scar Andrij had seen a hundred times. "Boz was a new king when it broke out, but with Jacek marrying Boz's sister, Natasza, he had to honor the alliance. We both know the king hates to look weak. I assume Jacek's the same."

"So much is resting on a chief's pride, then."

Valentyn laughed and laid his head against the wall, staring up at the thatched ceiling. "Boy, *everything* has always relied on chiefs' prides." His gaze flicked to Andrij for a moment. "Ya should get on that horse of yours and go. Appreciate the sentiment to stay and talk with your old mentor, but Boz will kill us both if you're late."

Andrij rose and grabbed Valentyn's forearm. As Valentyn returned the gesture, Andrij smiled. "I'll drink a few extra mugs of oskoła for you. Don't get too soft without me. Wouldn't want a woman to take away Astiw's best warrior."

"If I'm Boz's best warrior, we're all doomed." Valentyn unclasped his cloak and held it before him. "Take it."

"No." Andrij stepped back. "Those cloaks are for generals and heroes in war. I'm neither."

"Tell that to the people out there. To them, you're the Firebringer. If it doesn't feel right, ya can give it back to me in a few days. Better to let old Jacek see an Astiw rider in the right gear, though, eh?"

Without waiting for an answer, Valentyn threw the cloak to Andrij, who held it up, examining it in the candlelight. "This thing's obviously been through a lot of battles." Their own battle had left charred bits along the sides, and Andrij took pride in knowing he'd led the charge.

"And it'll see more," Valentyn said. "Now, go! Get that runt horse of yours and ride."

Ash coated the village when Andrij emerged from the cottage. The fires had been kept mostly to the trails, away from the buildings, but sections of the forest had gone up in the blaze. Though he winced at the sight of the damage, Andrij clenched his fists and held his head high. Every battle brought destruction. The Firebird's feather had saved Małe Wzgórze, and even if it would take time for them to recover, they wouldn't suffer as his family did. They had food and a well free of corpses, and now, no raiders would dare threaten them after the stories spread.

Beáta offered him a smile as he untied Oleh from a pasture fence. "I will take good care of him."

He nodded. "I know you will. Just keep an eye on him. Valentyn has a knack of eating a village's entire stock of verhuny."

"Those treats are called chruściki here," she said with a giggle, "but I fear we will not have desserts for some time. Thanks to you, though, we will not starve."

She swiftly returned to the woods, likely collecting any herbs that had peeked above the snow before the equinox. Andrij felt a bit of joy watching her go. Valentyn deserved to be happy, and with her, maybe he finally had a chance.

Oleh nuzzled his hand as he offered the horse a bit of grain. "C'mon boy, let's ride." There were still days to go, but after protecting Małe Wzgórze, Andrij sat straighter on Oleh's back. He wasn't a general or a hero yet. Someday, maybe he would earn the cloak on his shoulders. First, though, he would earn his freedom.

The day's travel west was quiet as Andrij pondered battles of the past. He had seen combat but never like the night before. This fight had been a success, but what if things had gone wrong? He had failed to fight by Valentyn's side, and now, his mentor was lying with a wound that may never fully heal. In his mother's tales of warriors, they never failed. It was a heroe's job to sacrifice for those around them and ensure none died.

"No prize in this life comes without struggle," she'd said. "Not the crops of the ground or the cloak over your shoulders. For some, the burden is lighter, but those raiders made sure ours would be as heavy as the yolk of a workhorse."

He sighed. It didn't matter. Hero or not, he would reach Dwie Rzeki and earn his freedom. *I'll be home soon, Mother.*

When night fell, Andrij struggled to keep Oleh on the narrow trail with only the crescent moon's light. Each tree seemed the same, and his progress slowed to a crawl as the gales picked up.

"Something isn't right," Andrij said to Oleh as he gritted his teeth and pushed the horse on. The east wind blew the storm, not the typical north or west. "It's an eastern wind, like the one that sent the last blizzard. Dziewanna said that Marzanna…"

Then he saw the two piercing blue eyes.

He'd hoped the wolf had stopped stalking him after the battle at Małe Wzgórze, yet here it was, watching. Why? With the wind whipping through his hair, he dismounted and pulled his spear. "What do you want?" he shouted. "Haven't enough died?"

The wolf growled, and Oleh whined behind Andrij as he advanced. Whether it be raiders, beasts, or the king himself, Andrij had always lived in fear of forces more powerful than him. But he was done being afraid.

"What do you want?" he demanded again, his voice sharp. "Speak or leave!"

For a moment, the winds calmed. A chill washed through Andrij, beneath his skin like the grip of a deadly illness. The wolf stepped forward. Its eyes bore into him, and it seemed to smile as a woman's voice pierced the night. "Your time will come, Andrij."

Then the wolf bounded into the woods, disappearing as quickly as it had come. Before Andrij could call after it, the storm returned. He scowled and gripped his spear. That voice… There had been power in it, like that he'd felt in Dziewanna's. Could it have been the goddess of winter herself?

Swiftly, Andrij mounted Oleh and kicked the horse into a gallop. He had no answers, but if he was to make it to Dwie Rzeki, he couldn't afford these distractions. Storm or not, he would ride through the night.

For days Andrij traveled west, only resting for an hour at a time when Oleh needed to drink.

The stubborn horse had served him well on the journey, but both mount and rider were exhausted. So close to Dwie Rzeki, though, he had no choice but to charge on.

He still saw the wolf at times. It watched him from the shadows, never speaking again, but its message rang in his mind. What had it meant?

With a shake of his head, he pushed Oleh on, down the path to Dwie Rzeki. They weren't far now based on the number of scattered villages they had passed. Soon, he could sleep. He would deliver his message before slumping somewhere with far too many horns of oskoła to forget what he'd faced. Then, he would ride home.

It was late on the night of the equinox when the farms and cottages increased in number. By now, Andrij's mind had long numbed to both his thoughts and the sound of Oleh's hooves against the dirt, but when they reached Dwie Rzeki's eastern gate, he smiled.

Almost there.

Not all hope was lost. Though Mykyta had fallen and Valentyn had been wounded, Andrij clutched to Boz's promise. This had been the longest week of his life, but in the end, it would be worth it to see his family, his mother, again.

"Come on, Oleh!" he said, patting the stallion on his neck. "Let's finish this."

Oleh felt his excitement and burst down the trail to where the Wyzra and Krowik rivers met. It was the Drowning of Marzanna, and if the festival was still in full swing, they would surely be conducting the rituals representing the goddess's death. The smoke rising from the northwest confirmed his suspicions. He had made it in time.

Besides a couple sneaking away to disobey their parents, the trails were clear as Andrij neared the source of the smoke. A similar festival would be celebrated that night in Kynnytsia as well—the first Andrij would miss. Each year before his father's passing, his family had traveled to the capital for the spring equinox. Distant memories.

Crowds appeared as a fire flickered ahead. They screamed and scattered when Andrij passed, but he gave them no attention. The only Krowikie that mattered were the chiefs and the pair that Dziewanna had spoken of.

He'd wondered each day about who they were—the two who could stop Marzanna. Dziewanna had given little information, but he promised himself he would find them someday.

If Marzanna truly was plotting to defeat spring, then they were his tribe's only hope.

The trees split at the confluence of the two rivers, and Andrij leapt from Oleh's back as he entered the clearing, landing before a group of gawking women. But it was not they who drew his attention.

A boy and girl stood beneath the trees' shadows, apart from the crowd. The girl wore the traditional flower crown of the festival, but unlike most, her wreath and dress were white with black streaks instead of the bright colors others donned. She watched him with distrust. Her partner, though, had awe in his blue eyes. The Firebird feather burned in Andrij's pouch at the sight of the blond boy, as if it knew something he didn't.

But he was not here for speculation. There were hundreds at the confluence. Any of them could have been the pair, and besides, it was only his message that Dziewanna had claimed would begin their journey.

So he spoke.

"Where is High Chief Jacek Lechowicz?"

His voice hung in the air, only interrupted by murmuring and the crackling of the great bonfire. Then, the high chief stepped forward, his shoulders draped with fur of both wolf and bear and his eyes as piercing as the sharpest sword. "I am here," Jacek said.

Andrij swallowed as the high chief approached, but he continued as loudly as he could, "My name is Andrij Myroslavovych Yakymchuk, and I bring a message from your great ally Boz Vladyslavovych Kramarenko, king of the Astiwie. An army has amassed itself east of our lands. We are all in danger."

END OF THE RIDER IN THE NIGHT

Keep reading for an exclusive preview of book 1 in The Frostmarked Chronicles, A Dagger in the Winds.

A Word From The Author

Writing this prequel ahead of the epic journey of *A Dagger in the Winds* was a lot of fun, and I hope you enjoyed this preview into the life of Andrij. Be sure to keep an eye out for him throughout The Frostmarked Chronicles!

If you have enjoyed reading this story as much as I have writing it, please take the time to post an honest review on whatever retailer you purchased this book from (or wherever your favorite retailer is if you received the book as part of my newsletter). Every review helps new readers discover the series.

Be sure to read on for the first few chapters of *A Dagger in the Winds*. If you liked this story, I'm sure you'll love meeting Wacław and Otylia.

- Brendan

About the Author

Brendan Noble is a Polish and German-American author currently writing fantasy books based on Slavic mythology. He is fascinated with history, economics, and politics in both reality and fiction.

Brendan is a recent graduate in Economics from Hillsdale College in Michigan. Brendan began his writing career in November of 2018 with a challenge from his wife to complete National Novel Writing Month and has been an author ever since.

Outside of writing, Brendan is a data analyst and soccer referee. His top interests include German, Polish, and American soccer/football, Formula 1, analyzing political elections across the world, playing extremely nerdy strategy video games, exploring with his wife, and reading.

A Dagger in the Winds (Book 1 of The Frostmarked Chronicles)

Keep reading for a preview of the book.

Prologue

Wacław

We're going to be in so much trouble…

"WAIT FOR ME!"

I scampered into the moonlit woods, clutching my wool cloak in one hand and my makeshift spear in the other. It was nothing more than a poorly sharpened stick. In my mind, though, it was a mighty weapon, capable of killing the demons and monsters lurking in the shadows.

Otylia glanced back with a smirk. Her bright green eyes pierced the sea of white surrounding us as her breaths fogged the air. "Hurry up! Dziewanna waits for no one."

With a sigh, I hopped through the snow after her.

Otylia was my best friend, but all she'd wanted to talk about recently had been the wild goddess. Like me, she'd turned twelve last summer, and she would soon be initiated as a szeptucha—a channeler of the gods, capable of amazing sorcery. She wanted to be chosen by Dziewanna more than anything. I worried I was going to lose her.

"You're so much faster in your soul-form," she quipped, hopping over a log once I caught up. Her herb bag flapped against her leg as she ran, but even with the hindrance, she was quick. "Why don't you just stay in it?"

"I have to wake up *eventually*," I replied.

Whenever I slept, I emerged from my body in what we called my soul-form. I was invisible when I wanted to be but could interact with the world like normal. Mom and Otylia were the only ones who knew about it, and Mom had forbidden me from exploring at night. Tonight, though, was the eve of the spring equinox.

With Otylia's father, High Priest Dariusz, out late preparing the festival's rituals, Otylia had snuck to our cottage once Mom was asleep. I had slipped out to meet her.

This wasn't our first time wandering the dark woods, but tonight was supposed to be special.

The stories said you could *see* the spring gods as they traveled to kill Marzanna, goddess of winter and death. Dziewanna was among them, so Otylia had demanded we go.

I shivered as I leaped over another log. The snow had lingered unusually late this year, but Dziewanna and Jaryło, god of spring and war, would rid the world of it come morning. Part of me would miss its beauty.

"Where are you going?" I asked, stopping as Otylia ducked deeper into the forest. "Mom says there's demons away from the trails."

She stomped back to me with her nose wrinkled. Her long black hair, braided and wrapped in twine, swept behind her as she snatched my hand. "It'll be fine! Mother showed me the way to a grove in autumn. We'll be able to see Dziewanna flying from there."

"Why do you always talk about her and not Jaryło? He matters too."

Furrowing her brow, she pulled me along. "Because *he* gets all the attention from Father and the tribe. Dziewanna's the one that Marzanna can't kill in winter. She keeps the wilds alive during Marzanna's moons, but she's been forgotten by everyone except Mother and me."

We wandered on for a long time. I had no idea how she knew where she was going in the darkness. Though I knew much of the forest around our village of Dwie Rzeki, to me, every tree seemed the same this far from home. And with the clouds obscuring the stars, it was impossible to tell which direction we were headed.

The eight winds whistled through the branches above when we finally reached a small clearing.

Otylia grinned and twirled, swinging the skirt of her deep green dress around her. "Come on, Wašek!" she said, using the affectionate 'little' version of my name—Wacław—that only she and Mom called me. "Drop your spear and dance with me!"

"Of course, Otylka!" I replied with the same form of her name.

We danced hand-in-hand, spinning with the gales as they blew our hair and stung our cheeks until they turned red. Joy filled my heart. Otylia brought me the freedom I was too afraid to fight for by myself. With her, I felt like I could fly.

A growl ripped through the night.

I turned, placing myself between Otylia and the noise. My heart pounded as six pairs of ice-blue eyes glared at us from the trees. *Wolves.* They closed in, their snarling growing louder.

"Wašek, don't," Otylia said with a grip on my tunic's sleeve. "You can't fight all of them."

She was right, of course. But on the wolves' jaunt faces, I could see Marzanna's winter had been hard on them. They were hungry. Both of us would die if I didn't do something.

"Run," I whispered.

Otylia screamed as I dove for my spear.

The wolves charged, but my hands found the spear's shaft. The first wolf's jaws raced toward me as I swung its tip. Wood struck flesh, and with red streaking from its throat, the wolf yelped and fell, dead.

What did I just do?

The strike was just instinct. I had never wielded a real weapon before, let alone hunted something larger than a rabbit. My breaths shortened as my stomach churned. *So much blood...*

"Wašek!"

I spun as the other wolves charged, angered by the first's death. They came from every side. Their sleek white fur flashed through the shadows with the moonlight gleaming against their fangs. *There's too many.*

I stabbed at them as they reached me, but it wasn't enough. Teeth closed on my arms. Claws scraped my face and chest. I collapsed, screaming for Otylia to run.

Time slipped away. I prayed to Weles, god of the underworld of Nawia, to bring me paradise's peace. But death's release did not come.

A blast tore across the grove, flinging me through the snow as a brilliant light shone behind my eyelids. The wolves whimpered. My whole body shook against the frigid snow, the fear too much for me to look. Though the wounds were to my soul-form, when I awoke, the damage would remain on my physical body. So would the pain.

Eventually, the grove went quiet, and I gasped as I opened my eyes.

All six wolves lay dead, their bodies strewn amid a pool of blood that merged with the snow, staining it a deep crimson. Otylia stood at the grove's edge. Her fair skin glowed bright enough to illuminate the carnage, and her sharp green eyes were fixed on me. Horror filled them.

"What… What just happened?" I stammered, struggling to a knee as I clutched my throbbing torso. My head was woozy. Blood trickled down it and dripped to the ground. *Am I imagining this?*

Wide-eyed, Otylia stared down at her hands. "I think I just channeled."

A new fear struck me as I studied her. "How?" My best friend had channeled before being chosen by a god. What did that make her? I tried to stand, but my legs failed. I fell as Otylia rushed to my side.

"I don't know." Her voice trembled as she tore open her herb bag and pulled out a small clay poultice. "Just stay with me. Mother's healing salve should help."

I took her hand as my mind began to drift. "Whatever you just did, Otylka, thank you."

"Stay awake, Wašek." Tears welled in her eyes. "Stay awake!"

My grip slipped. I tried to call her name, to beg for her help, but tiredness washed over me. With my last breaths, I met her glowing eyes one last time before I fell into the black.

Part One

The Drowning of Marzanna

1

Wacław

FOUR YEARS LATER

He's winning… again.

"STOP HESITATING," XOBAS DEMANDED, circling me with sweat beading on his olive-skinned brow and his shield held tight to his chest. When he lunged, his cavalry sword clashed against my shield, knocking me to the dirt. "It's not your day, Wacław, is it?"

My arms ached as I pushed myself to my feet and sighed. *It's never my day when we're sparring.*

At Father's command, Xobas had trained me to fight ever since the wolf attack four years before. I was sixteen now. Still, the swordsman repeated the same instructions. Though Father believed his general's foreign style would teach me to adapt to any opponent, all it had given me was a sore butt.

A wicked grin crossed Xobas's face as he took his stance. "We go again. It's time for you to shake off the winter's chill and become the warrior the high chief expects you to be."

With a deep breath, I readied myself for the next blow, holding my wooden shield in front of me and my short spear alongside it. The cold shaft burned against my fingers. Despite the sun now hovering at the tips of the trees, its warmth had yet to reach our sparring ring.

"Why must we spar at first light?" I asked. "It's the equinox, and… you know…"

He advanced, chuckling as he did. "You Krowikie and your festivals. You believe this one is your time to find a girl?"

"Maybe…" I whispered to myself, unsure whether to hope as I thought of Genowefa dancing with the grace of the winds.

Xobas yelled and swung again, catching me in my thoughts. His sword sliced toward my head, and though I raised my shield to block the blow, the force was enough. I stumbled before he swept my legs and sent me to the ground.

His jagged gaze met me as I picked myself up for the fifth time that morning. "You can't be distracted like that in a battle," he said. "Solgawi swordsmen won't spare you if you let down your guard thinking about a girl's pretty eyes. In solo combat, you must take charge, understanding how your opponent will react."

I had grown up listening to warriors telling stories of Solga's many invasions from west of the Krowik River. Our tribe was named after that great river, and only it and a few miles of swampland separated their latest advance from our territory. Father had spent his life as the high chief working to unite the other Krowikie chiefs against the Solgawi. That unity had been enough to maintain peace for the last six years, but warriors in Father's inner circle were demanding we retake our lost land. I could only hope cooler heads prevailed.

Xobas's words spurred me. Despite my body aching from the beating, I gripped my spear tighter. He smiled as I shuffled forward, bending my knees so the circular shield covered more of my torso.

While he danced back and forth, I waited for my moment. I had seen this game far too often. He wanted to throw me off balance and strike the opposite direction. This time, I promised myself that I wouldn't let him.

For only a second, he hopped to the left. *Don't flinch.* I held my position as he spun back around, using his momentum to swing the curved cavalry sword. His stomach flashed beneath his tunic as his shield lagged.

Now!

I thrust my spear through the gap, striking Xobas just under his ribs and sending him to the ground.

As he wheezed and pushed himself to a knee, guilt swelled within me. The training spear had a blunt end, but he would be sore through the festival regardless. While he had given me more than my share of scrapes and bruises since we'd started sparring, I didn't enjoy hurting him.

"That's more like it!" he said, reaching his hand out to me as the light of Dadźbóg, god of the sun, split through the bare trees.

Grabbing his arm, I pulled him to his feet. He never covered his forearms, and on his right one, a tattoo of a horse traced the lines of a gruesome scar. I had always wondered if it had come from his time with the eastern Simukie clan before he'd joined our tribe. My curiosity had gotten the better of me once, but I had learned my lesson. Little angered Xobas. That question did.

"Have I earned myself a rest?" I asked, failing to hide my anticipation. There was much to do before the start of the two-day spring equinox festival surrounding the Drowning of Marzanna, but Father would be angry if I left before Xobas excused me.

Dirt covered his brown tunic, but he brushed it off without breaking eye contact. "Yes, you may go. It would be a shame if your gods struck me down for keeping you away from your *true love*." He chuckled. "Run along. Paint your pretty eggs and set your doll on fire."

"We're all part of the egg hunt, but only the girls paint them," I said, strapping my shield to my back and doing the same with the spear. "And it isn't a doll."

He sheathed his sword and crossed his toned arms. "Ah, yes. The burning and drowning of the winter goddess's effigy sounds like the perfect time to woo a beautiful woman."

He has a point. I blushed. "Won't you be coming? Last time I heard the stories, there was no age limit on having fun."

"But there definitely is on the belief in true love."

I shrugged. "Okay, suit yourself, but that just means more food for me."

With that, I took off, racing and sliding through the trees. In our settlement of Dwie Rzeki, there was nothing to do but farm, herd the cattle and horses, and wander the forest. There had to be *something* more.

As much as I didn't want to put my faith in a silly festival to fall in love, I would jump the fire tonight and be declared a man, eligible to wed. Our tribe considered the rituals of the summer festivals to be the peak time for couples, but the courting began now.

My doubts slid away with every second that passed. Just the thought of it made me giddy. *I listen to Mom's stories too much.*

Brown and gray ruled the forests, but today, the spring gods came with the dawn. Jaryło would bring life to the crops and his golden shield to protect us from our enemies, and Dziewanna would make the wilds bloom and rivers flow.

Each of my steps crunched more of the dried and dead leaves that had been preserved beneath the snow. I leaped with each landing, trying to crush as many of them as I could. Mom always said the forest, not the village, was our home. As

I listened to the trees creak in the wind and the leaves crinkle under my boots, I had to agree.

I reached the farmland at the edge of the village and jumped over a log, feeling the breeze skim the back of my neck. The cattle watched me run, but they paid me only a moment of attention before returning to their grass. *Just like the girls.*

With the trees sparser here, the daylight illuminated the sloped thatch roofs of the wooden houses, sunken below ground to keep in as much warmth as possible during the long winter moons. Besides the sound of my heavy breaths, the winds, and my boots thudding against the dirt, it was silent. I treasured that as I turned down the trail to our home.

There was something magical about the woods beyond Dwie Rzeki's wooden walls. They brought a peace that the day's work and busy village center lacked. With nobody around but the trees and birds, I was myself.

That magic faded as I passed the place Otylia and I had entered the forest four years before. Our final late-night journey. My heart ached at the thought. So much had changed since then.

A trail of smoke stretched to the sky ahead of me. *Mom's up.*

She was always an early riser, which made life difficult for me. While she found her energy from the second her eyes opened, I struggled to find that morning spark. My nightly wanderings in my soul-body stole that from me.

I hopped down the four steps to our house and pushed open the wooden door. It creaked as I slid inside, setting my shield and training spear on the dirt floor in the corner as the warmth of the stone stove washed over me. The house was only eight strides long and half that wide, so the stove never failed to keep us warm, even in the midst of winter's grip.

Mom turned from her kettle and smiled, the blaze illuminating her pale skin and loose golden hair. "I was wondering how long Xobas would keep you. Here, I'm sure you're freezing."

She handed me a steaming bowl of soup, which I accepted eagerly. As she went about making one for herself, I sat at the small table in the middle of the room and wrapped my hands around the clay bowl, letting its heat flow through my body. For just a few seconds, I didn't care that it burned my palms. "It took some effort to convince him to let me go this early."

"Your father will be pleased he's pushing you," she replied, sitting across from me.

All my life, she'd referred to him as *your father.* I assumed it was because Father had agreed to the request of High Chieftess Natasza that he throw us out of the longhouse, ending Mom's time as a concubine—a secondary wife. I had only been a baby when it'd happened. In a village with little in the name of drama, though, it had apparently been talked about for moons.

I didn't mind living apart from Father, Natasza, and my five half-brothers and sisters. Mom and I had a cottage to ourselves. We'd been forced beyond the village walls' protection, but Father's longhouse wasn't far. Just distant enough to typically avoid Father's stern control and close enough to see my siblings—or at least the ones I liked.

I stared at my spoon as it drifted through the steaming liquid. "I doubt my fighting will ever satisfy Father."

"Jacek is a difficult man to please." Her gaze dropped to her bowl before she smiled up at me.

Even with nothing but the stove's aura and the flickering candle on the table to provide light, her eyes were a bright blue like mine. *She's faking joy for me.* I let her do it. She wanted me to be happy, but she deserved it too.

"Are you excited for the festival?" she asked.

My heart jumped. I forced myself to sip the soup to give me time to think. All that accomplished, though, was burning my tongue, and I let out a yelp.

"Oh, that nervous?"

I wiped my mouth on my sleeve as I blushed. "Is it that obvious?"

"No, just a mother's intuition. Is there a girl in particular who has your heart fluttering like the birds? Genowefa? Otylia?"

How does she always know? All the boys wanted Genowefa. One glance from her was enough to make my heart stop. "Does it matter who I'm fond of? Father will probably just marry me off to some chief's daughter to keep his loyalty, and he's made sure I haven't had a real conversation with Otylia in years."

An understanding smile crossed her face. "I remember jumping the fire with hope in my heart." Her eyes drifted to the stove. Memories swirled in them. "Jacek was the second-born, like you, and all the girls were fond of him."

"Not like me…" I mumbled.

Chuckling, she reached across the table and squeezed my hand. It was a small thing, but it calmed my heart. "Oh, my Wašek," she began. "I would not wish upon you the trials your father faced. With prestige, it's often difficult to know who truly loves you and whose heart is full of greed. The others may scoff at you because of me, but when you find someone who sees beyond that, you'll know they're the one."

I picked at the calluses on my palm, avoiding her gaze. Being the son of a concubine didn't make me untouchable, but it was enough. Though I was Father's second-born, my family name was Lubiewicz, son of Lubena, instead of Jackiewicz, son of Jacek. Only bastards took their mother's name, and even now the other boys mocked me for it. To them I was the Half-Chief and nothing more.

"But you loved him?" I asked.

"It was hard not to. Your father could charm any girl, but at the summer solstice that year, he chose me." Her spoon slipped into the bowl. She stared at it for a few moments before letting out a sigh. "Of course, you have heard the rest of the story."

With a reassuring smile, I shrugged. "He got stuck with wicked Natasza, and you got me to help feed the horses and plow the field."

"And I thank Mokosz for that blessing." She tapped the wooden amulet of the Great Mother that hung from her neck, then stood without finishing her soup. As she pulled her dress from around the stool, she glanced at the stove and clicked her tongue.

During our meal, the fire had dwindled, and sorrow filled her eyes when she turned back to me. "I'm sure you would like to prepare for the festival, but can you grab more firewood first? They needed so much for the bonfire, and I—"

"Happy to," I said as I followed her to the stove. "There's still time before everything begins, and I'll never turn down an excuse to wander the woods."

"Don't travel too far, and don't—"

"Follow the leszy's whispers," I interrupted again, grabbing the iron ax leaning against my bed, where she'd probably placed it as a hint— one I had missed. Mom had constantly warned me of the forest spirit's call for years. Not that either of us had ever heard it.

She swept across the room, placing the bowls next to the bucket of water by her bed that she must have already pulled from the well. "I sometimes forget how old you've gotten."

I kissed her on the cheek and headed to the door with the ax swung over my shoulder. "Never too old to love your stories. Be back soon."

"When you return, I'll likely be feeding the animals. I love you."

I flashed a smile in response and climbed back into the daylight. Overhead, the eight winds carried the gray clouds, and I prayed to Perun, god of sky and thunder, that he'd stay his storms.

Please let me have this one day.

As I wandered through the woods, though, the air battered my back. I tried to ignore it as I searched for suitable downed trees to chop, but after a few minutes of enduring the torrent, I stopped and let the head of my ax rest against an exposed tree root. A chill ran up my arms.

"What are you telling me?" I asked Perun as I stared into the sky.

The bushes rustled nearby.

My breaths caught, and I whipped around, ready to fight as I studied the forest. Demons didn't often attack during the day, but other spirits lurked, and rogue wolves or bears could strike a lone wanderer. I shuddered. *Otylia can't protect me this time.*

A buck watched me from less than ten paces away, its eyes full of the fear I had felt moments ago. I loosened my grip on the ax. "Hey there."

It huffed and swung its head like a restless horse.

"What's wrong?" Deer weren't a rare sight, but they normally ran if you got too close. This one just stared at me and repeated the motion. *Is it trying to point?* I looked to the clouds. "You want me to follow it?"

The buck took off before skidding to a stop and looking back at me. It let out another sharp breath.

I glanced toward our cottage. *This isn't a voice, right?* A thrill rose within me as the winds returned, forcing me to stumble after the deer. Soon, I gave in and ran myself. What harm could a deer be?

Dashing through the trees, my arms and legs ached. I cursed Xobas for my soreness as the ax weighed me down. I struggled to keep up with the buck, but whenever it reached the edge of my vision, it stopped and waited, its eyes judging my slowness. "I'm coming!" I called after it.

Am I actually talking to a deer? Is that worse than talking to the sky?

Without answers, I kept running. The air seemed to chill the longer I went, and the ground grew hard against my boots as frost replaced the muck of spring. I knew the forest well, but by now, I had no clue where we were. Wherever the mysterious deer was leading me, I was trapped in its wake.

My patience soon wore thin and my legs tired. I stopped as we reached a rock outcropping, dropping the ax and placing my hands on my knees as I caught my breath. When I looked up, I lost it again.

The deer transformed, morphing into a spiraling tower of bark and leaves, roots and dirt. The creaking deafened me, and I froze to my spot as it grew to over twice my height. It twisted out, forming legs, arms, antlers, a mask of bone, and… *No…*

From the top of the tower, two green eyes stared down at me. A mouth formed among the vines, and the leszy's voice rumbled the whole woods when he spoke, "Hello, Wacław. I've been waiting for you."

www.ingramcontent.com/pod-product-compliance
Lightning Source LLC
Chambersburg PA
CBHW021254200726
48288CB00016B/3065